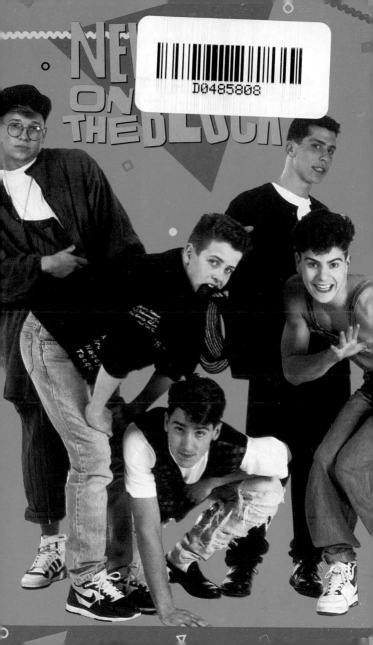

NE
ON
THE BLOCK

D0485808

THEY RACED FROM RAGS TO RICHES

They're five streetwise Boston kids, from hard-working families, who have skyrocketed to the top of America's pop charts. But what are they *really* like offstage and offguard?

▷ What would have happened to Donnie if he had stayed on the streets?
▷ What was it like to grow up as Jonathan and Jordan, in a huge family with an adopted brother and up to sixteen foster children?
▷ How has Joe balanced his deeply religious background with his show business success?
▷ What did Danny have to give up in order to join NEW KIDS?

All the answers to your questions are here, in the book you can't afford to miss!

THE LIVES AND LOVES OF
NEW KIDS ON THE BLOCK

JILL MATTHEWS

AN ARCHWAY PAPERBACK
Published by POCKET BOOKS

New York   London   Toronto   Sydney   Tokyo   Singapore

Front cover photo: Todd Kaplan/STAR FILE.
Cover insert photo: Janette Beckman/OUTLINE PRESS.
Back cover photos (L to R): Larry Busacca/RETNA LTD.,
Larry Busacca/RETNA LTD., Larry Busacca/RETNA LTD.,
Todd Kaplan/STAR FILE, Eddie Malluk/ RETNA LTD.
Cover and cover insert designs by Amy King.

AN ARCHWAY PAPERBACK *Original*

An Archway Paperback published by
POCKET BOOKS, a division of Simon & Schuster Inc.
1230 Avenue of the Americas, New York, NY 10020

ISBN: 0-671-72554-8

First Archway Paperback printing April 1990

10 9 8 7 6 5 4 3 2 1

AN ARCHWAY PAPERBACK and colophon are
registered trademarks of Simon & Schuster Inc.

Printed in the U.S.A.

IL 6+

Contents

Introduction

IN THE '40s, THEY SCREAMED FOR CROONER FRANK Sinatra. In the '50s, a fellow named Elvis swiveled his pelvis and drove the girls wild. The '60s brought "John, Paul, George and Ringo," the Beatles, while the '70s served up the Monkees, the Osmond Brothers and the Jackson Five.

Every generation of teenage girls has had at least one teen idol to call its own. As surely as the tide rolls in, so every few years another agelessly appealing band of boys rock their way into the hearts, minds, imaginations and, finally, memories of dreamy adolescents the world over.

Many tried in the '80s to fire the flames of teen passion, but none—not Duran Duran, the Bay City Rollers, Menudo—could keep that fire burning for very long. Until the end of the decade, that is. 1989 will surely go down in the annals of teen idoldom as The Year of the New Kids. In one fell pop-rockin' swoop, five boys from Boston filled that void and took center stage as the fastest-rising, hottest musical phenoms of the year—and they're rocketing right into the '90s, gathering momentum every day.

As every kid knows, New Kids on the Block are Donnie Wahlberg, Danny Wood, Joe McIntyre, Jonathan Knight and Jordan Knight, a quintet of talented, hard-working, clean-cut Kids who might have sprung from Any Block, USA to become *this* generation's heroes of the heart.

How much do their fans love the New Kids? Enough to buy an astounding *14 million* records in the USA alone in one year; keep their *Hangin' Tough* LP on the Top Album charts for a mind-boggling seventy-seven weeks; resurrect an old album that bombed when it was first released and make *it* a hit; put three LPs on the charts simultaneously *and* rocket six of their singles into the Top Ten in one year, a feat accomplished only once before in the decade, by superstar Michael Jackson.

New Kids fans bought well over a million copies of the group's two videos, *Hangin' Tough* and *Hangin' Tough Live in Concert,* catapulting them into the video-cassette-sales record books; they logged over 2.5 million calls to New Kids' 900-number phone line and kept the band's cross-country "Screaming Room Only" tour going strong for nine solid months, scooping up programs, T-shirts, posters, buttons and calendars along the way.

In early 1990, fans cited *Hangin' Tough* as their Favorite Pop/Rock Album at the American Music Awards and New Kids themselves as their Favorite Group. Those are pretty incredible statistics for a group they barely knew a year ago!

By now, the "Kidstory" has become legend. Certainly the faithful, and now even the casual chroniclers of pop culture, know that it all started way back in 1984 when producer/songwriter Maurice Starr and talent manager Mary Alford decided to put together a group of white teenage boys with "squeal appeal" who could rap, sing and dance. Maurice had had previous success with a group of black teens called New Edition (which spawned Bobby Brown), and when he broke ties with them, he figured he could do it again and, this time, corner more than just the black music market.

Casting the net in Boston, Maurice and Mary first hooked Donnie Wahlberg, a master rapper and Michael Jackson imitator who heard about the auditions through a friend and tried out, expecting nothing. Maurice and Mary loved everything about Donnie—his rapping, his dancing and, mostly, his charismatic personality and leadership qualities. They knew this Kid could be a star.

Failing to find others who measured up to darlin' Donnie, they asked *him,* "Any more like you in the neighborhood?" Donnie dug up his best buddy, breakdancer Danny Wood, and a couple of old friends from elementary school, singers Jonathan and Jordan Knight. All were accepted into the group.

In those early days, the fifth member was Jamie Kelly, another of Donnie's homeboy friends, but he didn't stay very long. By the summer of '85, Maurice and Mary decided they needed a much younger Kid to complement the others, one who could hit the high notes and, for want of a better comparison, be "the Donny Osmond or Michael Jackson" of the group. They found twelve-year-old singer/actor Joseph McIntyre and signed him on right away.

Maurice called his band of five Nynuk—to this day, no one knows why—and whipped them into musical shape, via *daily* music-and-dance lessons and nightly rehearsals. The Kids, still in school and even holding part-time jobs, worked hard. By 1986, through Maurice's connections, they'd landed a contract with Columbia Records, changed their name, and put out a self-titled debut LP. *New Kids on the Block,* the album, was a dismal failure; the group went back and tried again.

On the second try, they came up with *Hangin' Tough* and—powered by its hit singles "Please Don't Go Girl," "I'll Be Lovin' You (Forever)," "(You Got It) The Right Stuff," "Hangin' Tough," and "Cover Girl"—went straight to the top!

That's how the story goes—but, in reality, that's only a small part of the story. There's ever so much more that hasn't been told. Who are Donnie, Danny, Jon, Jordan and Joe really? What were their childhoods like, what "right stuff" do they possess that makes *these* five into the superstars they are today? Who are the people in their private lives? Who do *they* love? How is each one special, what unique qualities does each one bring to make New Kids kings of the pop/rock block? You're about to find out!

1

Donnie Wahlberg

NOTHING ABOUT THE BIRTH OF DONALD Wahlberg, Jr., was particularly extraordinary. In fact, Donnie's debut, back on August 17, 1969, was not very much different from the births of his three sisters and four brothers before him—an occasion of much joy for parents Alma and Donald Wahlberg, Sr.—but nothing anyone could point to about the tiny hazel-eyed bundle of joy proved, right from the start, that this one was different.

Named after his dad, he was called Baby Donnie, and he joined his big, happy family in their small home in the Dorchester section of Boston, Massachusetts. The new baby was doted on by his oldest sister Debbie, ten years old at the time, and had lots of built-in playmates, via sisters Michelle and Tracy plus big brothers Arthur, Paul, James and Robert. A few years after Donnie's birth, another brother, Mark, made the family complete. Besides playing with his sisters and brothers, Donnie had a favorite toy that was given to him when he was born: a soft and cuddly brown teddy bear that years later Donnie named "Teddy." He loved that stuffed animal more than anything, and he's still sentimental about it today.

The Wahlbergs did not have a lot in the way of material things. Donald, Sr., was "a union man," by Donnie's description, who drove a truck delivering food to schools and summer camps. Mom Alma worked as a nurse's assistant at nearby St. Margaret's hospital. The family owned their own small home, but luxuries were few and far between; clothing was routinely passed down among the children; having something new to wear to school was the exception rather than the norm. Christmas, in fact, was the one time the Wahlberg kids could count on something shiny and new for each of them—that's one of the reasons why Christmastime figures as Donnie's happiest childhood memory. "It would be hard to fall asleep the night before," Donnie remembers. "Then, about two o'clock in the morning, one of us would get up and wake all the others. We'd all gather at the top of the stairs and just sit there waiting for Christmas morning, getting all excited and hugging each other. Finally, when my parents would get up, we'd go crazy, fly down the stairs and the nine of us would start ripping open the presents!"

Looking back, Donnie's mom admits that there were hard times, times when they really could have used some extra money, times when a family vacation would have been nice —but that was something they could hardly ever afford. In fact, before New Kids, Donnie Wahlberg had been out of Boston only once, when the clan drove up to nearby Maine for a week. Still, what they lacked in finances, they more than made up for in love and family spirit. "When I think about it now," Donnie's mom relates, "I realize how hard it was, but back then, we never even realized it! We thought everyone had all these kids, everyone lived like this." The Wahlberg household was a busy, bustling one, filled with not only children but also pets of all varieties. While the kids were young, at least, they made their own family fun. Although it wasn't easy, with so many children, Mom Alma made sure dinners were always taken together—no exceptions to that rule!—and each child got to talk about anything on his or her mind. Donnie has always loved his mom's cooking—and his dad's, too.

The Wahlbergs also looked forward to their

weekly all-family bingo games, occasions that always produced lots of fun and laughter. Donnie loved playing—except when he didn't win, that is! That's when he sometimes let his temper get the best of him and ended up sulking in his room for the rest of the game.

But those occasions were rare for, by and large, the little blond boy with the straight-as-a-bowl haircut was a happy kid who got along well with everyone. Donnie was always closest to his youngest brother Mark; together, they withstood the bullying they sometimes got from their older brothers.

In those earliest years, Donnie stood out from his sisters and brothers as the child who played peacemaker among his huge clan. Donnie never liked to see anyone argue, and even though he was one of the youngest, he did his best to offer compromises and solutions. "Basically," Donnie remembers, "we'd fight over clothes, or who had the prettier girlfriend, which of us was the best athlete, stuff like that."

In fact, for a clan so large, the Wahlbergs were exceedingly close—back then *and* today, too! Perhaps one of the reasons is another activity the family always enjoyed together: church, every Sunday. The clan were parishioners at St. Gregory's church in Boston, and it was there, at the age of seven, that Donnie made his first holy communion. Church and family were, and are, strong threads in the fabric of Donnie Wahlberg's life.

Music was another thread in the young boy's life, though in the very beginning, Donnie probably wouldn't have said it was all that important. Music was just always *there,* compliments of his mom, Alma, a real music lover. She kept the radio or stereo on all the time, and since she liked all different kinds of music, the kids ended up being exposed to a little bit of everything. Donnie's mom was a bit of a ham, too, and once confessed to having showbiz aspirations of her own. Although she couldn't pursue her dream in any professional way, Alma was the first to sign on when her church staged musical productions as fundraisers. She was happiest when she was singing and tap dancing on stage. "I would come home from rehearsals," Alma remembers, "and wake everyone up so they could see my two new tap dance steps. I would be cookin' supper with my tap shoes on and I would make them come to my shows. Sit through them." And indeed, the whole clan dutifully trooped off to see their mom at each show, applauding her efforts loudly. But they never thought of it as anything special or different—it was just Mom, getting to do something she loved.

What *Donnie* loved, way back then, was not so much music, as sports. Along with his big brothers, Donnie was a real sports nut. Being a city kid, he played lots of basketball in the schoolyards, but baseball was his absolute favorite. One of Donnie's most cherished memories is playing baseball with his brothers Bob and Mark in a nearby park every spring and summer evening until sunset. He was very good and, like lots of little boys, used to dream about being a major leaguer one day. Back then, as now, Donnie rooted wildly for all the hometown teams—the Boston Bruins, Celtics, Patriots and, of course, the Red Sox.

As he grew older, Donnie was carving out his own little niche in the family. Along with his efforts as family peacemaker, Donnie was becoming the Wahlberg that other people seemed particularly drawn to, the one who was always the center of attention—and who loved being there. He began doing things just to get attention and became quite the little ham. It wasn't that he suddenly decided he wanted to get into showbiz: "I had show-*off* aspirations," Donnie would confide in an interview years later. "I never really dreamed of being a singer or a star, I just always wanted to be the center of attention." Still, as Donnie grew, the undeniable magnetism of his personality was getting stronger. Although he didn't admit it to any but his closest friends, Donnie was already fantasizing about becoming famous. "I didn't care whether I was just famous in my neighborhood . . . I used to love standing up and telling jokes to all my friends, having everyone laugh. I didn't really care if I made it for the whole world to see me, but I always felt that I had something the world would want to see."

The neighborhood of Boston that Donnie grew up in, Dorchester, was home to many different kinds of people. It was neither a wealthy suburb nor a run-down urban eyesore. Hardworking folks of all creeds and races lived harmoniously side by side and took pride in their homes. Still, racial harmony wasn't the case in all of Boston, and to try and remedy an educational system that seemed to favor the Caucasian majority, Boston began a program of busing kids to schools outside their neighborhoods. The idea was to improve the all-around quality of education by bringing white kids into minority schools and vice versa. Many people involved were not happy with this idea and fought hard against it. Others who could afford it simply put their kids in private schools and avoided the situation altogether.

The Wahlbergs were never in a position to send any of their children to private school; it was not an option they would have considered even if they had the means. For Alma and Donald, Sr., felt that sending their kids to a school in a different neighborhood could have a positive effect; after all, the real world is made up of many different kinds of people, and learning at an early age to get along with everyone could only be beneficial.

And so when it was time for little Donnie to start kindergarten, he hopped aboard the big yellow school bus that would take him to the William Monroe Trotter School in the section of Boston known as Roxbury. It was a long bus ride—over a half hour in each direction. But Donnie made friends on the bus and never minded the ride. Going to school so far away became a way of life he just took for granted. And, as his parents had hoped, going to school with kids of all backgrounds proved a wonderful learning opportunity for Donnie and all their kids! Today, Donnie says, "Being bused to school in Roxbury was the greatest thing that ever happened to us."

He's got good reason to feel that way. For it was during those early elementary school years that Donnie became exposed to the soul and rap music of his new black friends. He not only found he loved that kind of music, but he discovered a talent for it himself. Donnie found he was good, not only at repeating the rapping rhymes others had composed, but he was pretty good at making them up himself!

Donnie found another boy just his age who also loved rap music and was bused to the Trotter School from Dorchester. This boy's name was Danny Wood, and the two struck up a friendship that's still going strong today! Donnie and Danny would spend many an afternoon and evening composing little rap ditties—sometimes they did *that* rather than their homework. "We only let the rapping interfere with our schoolwork sometimes," Donnie admitted, but that was the one area where his mom really kept on top of him. Sometimes Donnie would leave his work undone and then get up early in the morning to try and polish it off! But this didn't affect the young boy's grades all that much, for Donnie was, if not the top student, certainly a good one. History was his best subject, mainly because it was something that interested him. And if Donnie was interested in something, he'd often go above and beyond the assignment just to learn other things about it. On the other hand, if he was studying something he didn't much care for, he did a minimal amount of work and let it go at that.

No matter how much or how little work he put into his class assignments, nearly all of Donnie's teachers liked him. He was a bit of a class clown, but not in a nasty, disruptive way. "He was a happy kid, never moody" was the consensus among his teachers. He was also very popular, and numbered among his friends were kids of all colors and creeds.

Music was beginning to take on more importance in young Donnie's life, especially the music that was so popular with his black friends. Donnie, however, was more into the rhythm and rhyme of it all—he never had the best voice, something he's the first to admit. "I was never really a singer," he confessed, "but I always liked to do anything that had to do with rhythm, dancing, rapping, or playing the drums." Not that Donnie ever *had* a real drum set to bang away on; it was always makeshift pieces that nevertheless kept him busy and happy.

Not having the world's greatest voice never bothered Donnie, since he could express himself musically by rapping, dancing and playing, but he *was* disappointed when, out of all his friends, he was not chosen to be in the Trotter School chorus. Danny Wood was picked and so were two brothers Donnie was just getting to know: Jonathan and Jordan Knight. "The Knight brothers had really good voices," Donnie remembered about them. That memory would come to play in a big, big way later on!

Donnie discovered something else about music that he loved; making it was a way to get attention, and that appealed to the young extrovert. So when Danny and his other friends were off at chorus practice, Donnie found a couple of guys and formed his own little group. "We called ourselves Risk,"

Donnie laughingly recalls, "and we were really terrible. Except we didn't think so. We played everything by ear, and sometimes if it sounded vaguely like it was supposed to, we thought that was great." Donnie, on his makeshift drum set, and his little band would practice playing and rapping under the front porch of Donnie's house—he was all of ten years old!

Donnie's burgeoning creativity was starting to express itself in other ways as well. He began to draw and soon was creating comic book characters and making up stories to go with his drawings. He also got into drawing graffiti, something he found he was very talented at. Whatever Donnie drew, or created, he kept, and before long, his room was papered with all his creations. It still is today—Mom Alma tattles that the only time Donnie's room is tidy is when he's on the road and she goes in and throws things out! Donnie's always been quite the collector; he's always loved the TV show "Sesame Street" and must have at least thirty Grover dolls, among other paraphernalia, all over his room!

After elementary school, Donnie, along with Danny, was enrolled in the Phyllis Wheatley Middle School, and while he continued to be a good student when he was interested, music began taking over more and more of his life.

For Donnie had found a musical idol to emulate: none other than Michael Jackson. Donnie thought Michael was the best, incredibly smooth and cool, from the singing star's jewel-encrusted glove to the tips of his pointy black moonwalking shoes. And Donnie copied it all—he saved up and bought himself a Michael Jackson look-alike red leather jacket, got the glove and the shades and the shoes, and taught himself to do a mean Michael moonwalk. Soon, Donnie was the best Michael J. imitator on the block! In fact, Donnie became known throughout Dorchester for his dead-on Michael Jackson impression.

When Donnie was twelve years old, a part of his world and his security came tumbling down. His parents decided to divorce and, suddenly, the family would no longer be together. His older sisters and two of his brothers were already out on their own; two other brothers were going to live with his dad, while he and younger brother Mark would stay with their mom. Although no one in the Wahlberg family has ever talked much about the breakup, it must have affected Donnie deeply; after all, he was the one to whom family peace meant so much. Donnie, Mark and Alma moved to a tall, narrow three-family home on a quiet, gently sloping street in Dorchester, not far from their first family household. It wasn't far, either, from Donnie's dad, and that was important, for Donnie is devoted to his dad and has always maintained a good relationship with him.

Even after the divorce, Donnie continued to see Donald, Sr., as often as possible, usually stopping by on the way home from school. And in the summertimes, when Donnie was a teenager, he worked side by side with his dad, helping with deliveries of food to summer camps and schools.

When his mom remarried a few years later, Donnie became close with his stepdad, Mark Conroy, while still maintaining very close ties with his real dad. In fact, when New Kids came along, both of Donnie's dads were as supportive and excited as his mom.

Donnie went on to Copley High School, where he continued with his interest in rap music and sports. He played baseball for the school team and began hanging out with a group of friends, including Danny Wood, who called themselves the Kool Aid Bunch. Although members of the group came and went, Donnie and Danny remained at the core and spent their time making up new rap routines. Soon, they were performing at parties. There, they discovered that girls *really* liked them. "And that was the main reason we continued," Donnie divulged, "not because we thought we'd be rap or dance stars someday, but just because it was really fun and we loved the girls screaming for us at parties."

It was during his high school years at Copley that Donnie developed another creative interest; he joined the drama club and found he really liked acting. He got to be in several plays before New Kids came along.

Donnie will be the first to tell you that at this point in his life, his midteen years, there were a lot of different influences around, not all of which were wholesome. Although he's private about discussing it, Donnie has admitted that some of his brothers had reputations as local tough guys; Jim shaved his head and at least one brother and one of his sisters had problems with drugs. And Donnie certainly was tempted himself.

"I'm a dude that could easily have turned to drugs and crime," Donnie revealed in a candid moment. "I could have ended up in jail. I was a real mischievous, defiant kid." What kept him from becoming just another statistic was *not* New Kids and the opportunities that afforded him. For even before New Kids came along and changed his life forever, Donnie Wahlberg looked around at what was happening to his sister and brother; he looked deep within himself and somehow, somewhere, found the strength to just say no to all the negative stuff around him. "I learned it was best not to do that stuff when I saw what happened to my family members. One day my mind said, 'Stop.' And I did." He found strength in being creative, in doing his music, his writing and performing and standing up for what he believed in.

It was Donnie's rapping and Michael Jackson–like dancing abilities that brought Donnie to the attention, one sultry summer day in 1984, of a friend who suggested he audition for this new group that was being formed by Maurice Starr and talent manager Mary Alford. Although Donnie didn't think he was really a good enough singer, and almost didn't go to the auditions at all, something made him change his mind. And that something has made all the difference.

For as the legend goes, once writer/producer Maurice Starr got a look at Donnie's dancing, rapping and leadership abilities, New Kids was officially born!

2

Jonathan and Jordan Knight

IF NEW KIDS ON THE BLOCK HAD NEVER COME along (what a thought!), it's still entirely possible the world would have heard from Jonathan and Jordan Knight anyway. Oh, maybe they wouldn't have grown up to be superstar pop singers, or even entertainers for that matter, but it seems sure they would have made their mark doing something remarkable. That's because they come from a truly remarkable family.

The brothers who helped put Dorchester, Boston, on the map were born into a family that's originally from Canada. Both sets of Jon and Jordan's grandparents, the Knights and the Putmans, live in the province of Ontario.

That's where Allan Knight, a carpenter by trade, and Marlene Putman first met and married. The couple, who were musically talented and instrumentally skilled—Marlene on accordion and Allan on guitar—settled in the Boston area and began to raise a family. They had three children of their own, Allison, Sharon and David, and an adopted son named Christopher (who is black), before Jonathan Rashleigh Knight was born in Wooster, Massachusetts, on November 29, 1968. Jonathan, who's sometimes uncomfortable with that weighty middle name—it's his grandma's maiden name—was a quiet, shy little baby, most of the time, anyway. "But when he got your attention," his mom relates, "he wouldn't let you go for hours, he just kept wanting *more* attention!" Jonathan had no trouble fitting into the growing Knight clan—and Mom Marlene had lots of help with him from Allison, who was eight at the time of Jon's birth, and Sharon, nearly six. But it would be Allan and Marlene's next child that Jonathan would grow closest to. In fact, Jon says today that he and Jordan were brought up almost like twins. "We were never apart."

Jordan Nathaniel Marcel Knight made his appearance on the sunny spring day of May 17, 1970, and just like the season, Jordan's personality, right from the start, was light, breezy, calm and refreshing. Jordan had big chubby cheeks that were always rosy, puppy-dog wide brown eyes and a head full of thick, black, curly hair. "I called him my enchanted one," his mom has said, because Jordan turned out to be as sweet as he was beautiful. He was the kind of baby everyone fell in love with—come to think of it, that's not very different from the Jordan we know right now!

The Knight family was a big one, but they never did have a lot of money. Allan Knight gave up his carpentry job to become a minister; Marlene Knight, a college graduate, became a social worker. In the family's very first home, the four little boys shared *one* bunk bed, with Jon and Jordan on the top and David and Christopher on the bottom. It was tight, especially when you added the ever-present cats and dogs the family counted as pets. Still, no one really thought they were poor, and, indeed, what they had in family love was worth more than all the riches in the world.

When Jordan was about four, the family moved. They found a wonderfully huge house on a modest but lovely street in Dorchester that would more than satisfy their family's needs. The house was an old seventeen-room Victorian, complete with ten bedrooms and four bathrooms. It was set way back from the street—the only house on the block like it—which afforded the family a giant front yard for the kids to play on. Although the house was uniquely roomy, especially in a neighborhood of small, ranch-style houses, that didn't mean the Knights had suddenly become the rich kids on the block. For the house was not exactly in tiptop shape; there was a lot of fixing up the family had to do and a lot of upkeep once they moved in. The bright yellow paint was constantly peeling, the immense lawn was always in need of mowing, the plumbing was sometimes leaky.

Still, the house was in a neighborhood that was great for kids. It was only a block away from the stores, so it was easy for any of the Knight kids to run errands. There were families of all nationalities around, and even if there were no nearby baseball fields, a pickup basketball game could always be arranged on the street. In the summers, Jon fondly remembers opening fire hydrants near the house and jumping in and out of the streams of cool, clear water.

The house, also, wasn't too far from the Boston "T"—the subway, that is—that could take family and friends into the city or to the surrounding suburbs. And that's pretty much how Jon, Jordan and their bunch got around— by public transportation, no fancy cars for them!

You'd think that moving into such a grand home would have given the Knight brothers lots of room to spread out. Yes, each kid got his own room ("Mine was the smallest," youngest bro Jordan has reminded people), but, astoundingly, there was never a time when the Knights were alone in the house. There was never a time when it was just the eight family members rambling around in that big old house.

For over the years Marlene Knight had become extremely active in her career and, at one point, was the director of a group home for adolescents. At that time, she made a humanitarian decision that would affect the lives of her family forever. With her husband's approval, Marlene decided to take in foster children to live among her family. The kids were of all ages—later on, some were even foster adults. —and she never took in just one or two. At any given time, the Knight household swelled to between sixteen and eighteen people living under one roof!

There are very few families who, especially with six kids of their own, and very little money, would even think of doing what Jon and Jordan's did—but their mom's simple, honest feeling was "These kids needed homes. Someone had to provide them. Why not us?"

And although there were times when Jon, Jordan, Allison, Sharon, Christopher and David probably felt, "Well, why can't it be just us?", for the most part, they adapted incredibly well to their extended family situation.

25

They learned to share not only toys but also clothes, food, homework, ideas, thoughts, feelings and just about everything, with an ever-changing cast of new brothers and sisters. They learned firsthand that kids are not always born healthy, that kids are not always born loved. They learned that while they didn't have a lot of money, there were many others in the nearby world who had much less. That's one of the reasons Jon and Jordan are so sensitive to New Kids fans and one reason why they'll *never* be stuck up! "We learned to get along with all kinds of people," they understated.

As Jon and Jordan remember it, having so many people in the house made for some very creative fun times. Everyone would band their toys together and create little villages, make up silly scenarios, write and direct little plays that their toys "starred" in. Of course, there was the usual squabbling over territorial rights, but much less than you might expect. "Our mother's attitude and loving way definitely rubbed off on us," they say. And that's a key to their true personalities today!

Since there were so many kids in the house, Jon, Jordan and the crew learned early on to attend to their own chores. After all, the family was hardly in a position to hire cleaning help and no one person could be expected to do it all. So the guys got used to doing their own laundry, cleaning their rooms and—Jon's special task—mowing that expansive front lawn! They also got pretty good at being independent in the kitchen. Jon can cook—"Anything I want," he says—while Jordan's a master at peanut butter and jelly sandwiches. But no one seemed to mind the housework especially; it was a way of life, the only one they knew.

In spite of having so many children around, each person's birthday was cause for a very special celebration. "We could always count on a cake, presents and *everyone* being there to help celebrate," Jordan remembers. "It was the one day that was your special day alone."

Christmases were special, too. Of course there was always a tree and each family member got his or her own stocking hanging on the mantle. Both Jon and Jordan have told reporters about their fondest Christmas memories. Here's Jon's: "I don't remember how old I was, but I was still sharing a bed with Jordan, so it must have been a while ago. We had this big old brick fireplace in our house and every Christmas we had a fire going in it. Well, one year my father took a pair of boots and tracked ashes from the fireplace leading over to the Christmas tree. I'll always remember that because, when I saw the footprints on Christmas morning, I was sure there was a real Santa and he had been at our house!"

Jordan's favorite Christmas memory was back during a Boston blizzard when all the stores in the area were closed. "Except this one store," Jordan recalls. "I heard this market was actually giving away food. Since my family wasn't real rich, we got out our sled, walked through the snow to the store, got some groceries and brought them back to our family. We had a nice Christmas dinner that year!"

To a large degree, family life for the Knights also centered around church. The family was active in Boston's All Saints Episcopal Church, and they spent a lot more time there than just attending services on Sundays. Church is where a deep-down fundamental love of music took root with all the Knights, but most especially, as you can guess, with Jonathan and Jordan.

For their particular church had a strong choir and all the Knight kids were part of it, except for Christopher, who wasn't particularly musical but was active in the church in other ways. Jon and Jordan, however, took to that choir like little fish to water, and it wasn't long before the choirmaster noticed their impressive vocal skills. Jon had a beautiful voice and he could pick up new music right away; Jordan was so turned on by the music that he was singing in choir before he could even read!

The choirmaster became good friends with the Knight family and took to working with Jon and Jordan on their vocal skills several days a week after school and before Mass on Sundays. It took a lot of dedication and determination to stick with a rigid schedule of so much practicing, but both Knight brothers turned out to be very determined, especially when it came to music! To this day, Jon and Jordan credit that choirmaster with being their first and most important musical influence. "He taught us almost everything we know about music," Jon allows.

It wasn't long before the Knight brothers were co-leaders of their church's choir and they even spent one summer at a special program for selected boys whose vocal promise was outstanding.

Although their mom, and to be sure, that choirmaster, recognized the boys had talent, neither Jon nor Jordan really thought seriously about where that musical talent could take them. "We sang because we loved to sing," they both agree, not because they were actively dreaming of being singing stars one day. Jon was a good writer, who once won an award for composing a Christmas story about Santa Claus; his first ambition, however, was to become an architect. He's secretly admitted that he used to "sing into the mirror and stuff, and maybe dream a little. But I never thought it would really come true." Besides, Jon was always the shy brother who frankly didn't have a lot of confidence in his abilities. On those fleeting occasions when he gave fame a thought, he always placed himself "in the background. There were times when I secretly wanted to be famous, but I always wanted to stay in the background!"

Jordan, with his distinctive high-pitched falsetto voice, freely admits he was *afraid* to consider pop stardom. "I was afraid that people would be in my business and guys would be jealous and hate me!"

Like the other kids in their neighborhood, Jon and Jordan were zoned for school in an area of Boston called Roxbury, about a half-hour's bus ride from where they lived. Their parents were actually happy about the situation, understanding that the school the boys would be going to, the William Monroe Trotter School, had an excellent academic reputation. And sure enough, Jon, and then Jordan, really flourished in the school.

Jon was a good student who expressed himself really well in writing. Jordan, though he doesn't read much now, used to be an all-star reader, plowing through several books per week. He even won a school award one year for "most books read" in his grade. Both Knight brothers made the school's chorus and made a lot of friends, those who lived in the neighborhood and others who were bused there. Just as they learned from the foster kids who came to live with them, so Jon and Jordan learned from the black kids they went to school with. They got into rhythm 'n blues music, rapping and the kind of street dancing that their school peers were mastering. It was at the Trotter School that Jon and Jordan met and became friends with Danny Wood, who was also in the chorus, and Donnie Wahlberg, a schoolmate who was not. Although the Knight brothers and Donnie were not the best of friends, as we all know now, their paths would certainly and happily cross again, just a few years later.

Summers for the Knight brothers were divided into trips to their grandparents in Canada—who sometimes rented a cottage on a nearby beach—and spending some weeks at church camp. Other lazy, hazy summer days were spent, as city kids often do, hanging out on the streets with friends, picking up the rhythms, vibes and fads of all that goes on out there. Although both Jon and Jordan describe themselves as "street kids, city kids," they, unlike Donnie Wahlberg, did not seem to be headed for trouble in any way.

Trouble found them, however, in the place they might have least expected it. In 1983, their parents, Marlene and Allan, who'd been having problems, decided to get divorced, and their dad left the big house they'd spent so many happy years in. Neither Knight brother has talked publicly about that dark time in their lives, but it must have affected them profoundly. For they did not go on to keep ties with their dad; they don't—"And it's our decision," they tell you—keep in touch with him. He has no part in the success of New Kids on the Block; in fact, Jon and Jordan almost never speak of him at all. When they're asked general questions about their parents, they only talk about their mom. In fact, they seem to have gotten even closer with Marlene in the last several years.

As the boys hit their teen years, their distinct personalities and interests began to emerge a bit more. Jon remained the quieter, more thoughtful, big-brotherly type, always, almost instinctively, looking out for Jordan. Although music and church was still a big part of his life, Jon began to take pleasure in simple things he could do with his hands. Carpentry and gardening became his two favorite "quiet time" hobbies. He wallpapered and decorated his bedroom, in addition to sanding the floor and painting Jordan's room as well! And Jon enjoyed not only gardening but also taking care of the lawn and the property, too. Even now, he admits, "I can't see paying someone else to mow the lawn when I can do it perfectly well myself!"

Creative, easygoing Jordan got even more into music when he hit his teen years. He fell in love with the music of the old soul group the Stylistics and began teaching himself to play the keyboards.

At the time, the big craze on the streets of Boston was breakdancing; Jordan found he was a natural mover. He'd spend hours after school perfecting his breakdance moves, learning new steps and once even spent a summer as a camp counselor teaching those moves to little kids. That training—learning and teaching others—would come in very handy, sooner rather than later!

When it came time for junior high school, Jon and Jordan were originally enrolled in the Phyllis Wheatley Middle School—that's where Donnie and Danny went—but through the influence of their church choirmaster, they went to a private school outside of Boston called the Thayer Academy. Although academically the boys continued to do well, that was the stage in Jordan's life, at least, when he sowed his wild oats. No, he never stole anything or got in with a bad crowd or anything like that, but he did become quite the graffiti artist, spray-painting his name on subway cars and sides of buildings all over town. It was his way, perhaps, of being creative, but, luckily, an even better way was about to come along.

For when Jon was sixteen and Jordan only fourteen, they got a message from their old elementary school buddy, Donnie Wahlberg: "This dude is looking to form a group and he wants you guys to audition."

When Jon and Jordan went to that fateful audition in the summer of 1984, and met Maurice Starr and Mary Alford, they didn't even tell their mom about it. And though the Knight brothers got in right away, it took quite a bit of time before Marlene was convinced that this musical group was something she was going to let her boys become involved with. Luckily, of course, she eventually did (she even went as far as allowing the fledgling group to rehearse in her basement), for what would New Kids on the Block be without those gorgeous—and as you now know, sensitive and very *special*—Knight brothers, Jonathan and Jordan!

Danny Wood

IT WAS A FINE SUNNY DAY IN MID MAY OF 1969 when Elizabeth and Daniel Wood, Sr., brought a new baby home from the hospital. This child was not their firstborn, but he was a first of sorts—after having three lovely daughters, the whole family was thrilled that there was finally a little boy in the house. He had dark hair with just a hint of a curl, big dark brown eyes and, when he smiled, the deepest, most darling dimples you could imagine.

They named him Daniel, Jr., after his own dad, and gave him the middle name William, after his mom's father. Right from the start, this baby boy was doted on by his big sisters, including Bethany, who was five at the time,

Melissa, four, and even little Pamela, three. He was always called Danny (to differentiate between him and Dad Dan), and although he was an active, mischievous little "live wire," he was mostly obedient. He loved to play with his first, most precious toy, a Teddy Bear puppet. "I still have that puppet," Danny says nostalgically, "and it still works. It's kind of an antique now." That sentimental side of his personality was evident early—and he's still the New Kid who's the most sentimental.

Danny's dad worked for the U.S. Post Office as a mail carrier, and in later years, when all the kids were in school full-time, his mom took a job as an administrative assistant for the Boston School Committee. Although Elizabeth, also called Betty, is not a teacher, her background and interests are strongly in the educational field. Making sure the members of her family got good educations was a high priority on her list.

The Woods family was not a wealthy one by any standards, but they were able to afford their own two-story home in the Dorchester section of Boston. The house itself, an old Victorian, which sits on the corner of a relatively busy street, was not particularly large, and when the family was complete, with the births of Danny's younger brother Brett and his baby sister Rachel, it had barely enough room for all eight busy, active Woodses. There were winters when the house was in need of better insulation and replacement windows that the family couldn't always afford, but the love and closeness of the clan generated their own special kind of warmth that no money in the world could buy.

All his life Danny has shared a bedroom with his brother Brett. The boys had bunk beds and Danny always slept on the bottom. It's hard to believe, but until very recently, even after New Kids was a smash success, Danny continued to share that room with Brett— and the superstar still found himself on the lower level of his boyhood bunk bed, even at twenty years old. That has only partly to do with the fact that he's been too busy to find more sumptuous quarters; mostly, it's because Danny simply enjoys being with his family and has never minded sharing a bedroom with Brett.

In fact, all the Woods kids got along well. As soon as his younger siblings were born, Danny, who'd been babied by his older sisters, took on the role of big brother enthusiastically. He loved watching out for Brett and Rachel and taking care of them. Danny has always been very open with his parents, too, and has never felt afraid to tell them exactly what was on his mind. To this day, in fact, Danny is extremely loyal to his clan and is one of the most family-oriented Kids you'll ever meet.

Perhaps one reason is that, like the other New Kids, family life centered around church. The Woods are of the Catholic faith, and they attended St. Ann's Church in Boston each and every week. And *all* the kids, not just Danny, sang their hearts out in the choir. No one thought any of the kids had any extra-special musical talent, but for the Woods, singing was a way of life—in church, in school and just around the house, for the simple joy of it. Neither Danny nor his sisters and brother ever thought about becoming a singing star.

Aside from church, there were other traditions Danny grew up with and holds dear. Even though there were six kids in the household, each child's birthday was a special occasion. "We made big events out of birthdays," Danny remembers. "We each got to pick what our favorite cake was and Mom would make it, and everybody joined in the festivities. You wouldn't want to miss someone's birthday at our house. It was just too much fun."

Christmas was another traditional family time at the Woods' home, and like the other Kids, Danny has a special memory and a silly secret. "I used to be afraid of Santa Claus," he's confessed. But that was when he was very young. Later on, he wasn't afraid to ask the big guy for the special toy he wanted. "My favorite Christmas memory was when I was seven years old and I got the Fisher Price Sesame

Street set. It had Big Bird, Oscar in the garbage can . . . the whole thing. I had been asking for it for months and months and I finally got it." Danny adds that, no matter what, Christmas is the one time he can count on seeing his entire family together. And that's even more meaningful now that he's hardly ever home. Even though two of his older sisters have moved out, he knows he'll definitely see them around the tree at Christmas.

Another of Danny's most cherished childhood memories is the big vacation his clan all took together one year. Although the family did not have a big bank account, one year they did manage a trip to Disney World in Orlando, Florida. That made such an impression on young Danny that it remains his favorite place on earth. Even now that he's traveled all over the world, when asked where he'd like to vacation, the first place he thinks of is Disney World!

When Danny was ready to start school, Boston had begun its busing program and the family received word that he would be attending the William Monroe Trotter School in Roxbury. Although their section of Dorchester was primarily Irish-Catholic, Danny's parents were not concerned in the least about their son going to school with kids of different racial backgrounds. "If anything," his mom has said,

"We thought it would be good for him to learn to get along with all kinds of people."

And, indeed, that's exactly what happened. For Danny Wood really flourished in school, and starting from kindergarten, it was clear that this Kid really had a good head on his shoulders. And when he put his mind to it, he could be a truly excellent student. Which most of the time he was—except for certain transgressions. Danny remembers one in particular: "In third grade we used to do these things where if you did enough work, you would get free time. And when the teachers checked your books, they would just look and see if you'd done it; they wouldn't check the answers. So I would write anything down to get free time! I did it so much, they finally caught me, so I got all *F*s on my report card and I had to make up all the work! It was real bad! I cried when I got caught!" As well he should have—Betty Wood was a sweet, understanding, but no-nonsense parent, especially when it came to schoolwork. The major disciplining, however, was left to Dan Wood, who every once in a while (though not too often) grounded his firstborn son for infractions of the family rules.

Those were rare occasions, though, for Danny had no trouble with school and less with the new friends he was making there. His first and best friend was the sandy-haired kid he met on the bus going to and from school, fellow Dorchester dude, Donnie Wahlberg. The boys lived fairly close to each other, though not within walking distance. It's safe to say that had they not been bused to school together, they might never have met!

Danny and Donnie found they had a lot in common. Both adapted well to their school environment and quickly made friends of all races and backgrounds. Both were interested in music and loved listening to the rhythm 'n blues sounds their schoolmates were into; both found they were good at picking up the steps of street dancing. Their only tiny elementary school rift came when Danny Wood was chosen as part of the school's chorus—and Donnie Wahlberg wasn't. It didn't do any permanent harm to their relationship. It was in the school chorus that Danny met and became friends with the Knight brothers, Jonathan and Jordan.

Danny's mom remembers going to several school performances that her son was in. "The school had what you would call a swing chorus," Betty Wood recalls. "They had a very fine musical director. I remember going to several performances that were held outside of school, in other parts of the city. Danny was active in that."

Once he went home, however, in those elementary school days, Danny didn't hang out with chorus buddies Jon and Jordan but, rather, spent a lot of time with Donnie and his other neighborhood friends. Danny did lots of the normal things growing up—none of which you could really point to and say: "Aha! He's going to become a superstar one day!" Not that Danny never dreamed of becoming famous. He's admitted, "I was this nearsighted, day-dreamy kind of kid. I dreamed of being famous, but I wasn't really sure at what, maybe a TV actor or something." He didn't really pursue showbiz in any way in those days though. Like his friends, he spent his after-school hours and weekends bike-riding around the neighborhood, going to lots of movies, especially adventure and horror flicks, although candid Danny will admit to being scared silly by those thriller-chillers.

While Danny was a basically easygoing kid, he did have a reputation for being a bit stubborn, for having a sometimes too-quick temper but mostly for being assertive and sticking up for his values and for his friends. He was never the biggest talker, but when something was important, he'd be the first one to speak out.

Aside from school, music and hanging out with his friends, Danny's all-consuming passion throughout his childhood was sports. Compactly built and muscular, Danny was a *good* athlete, so good his mom really thought he could go pro one day. Danny played basketball and soccer, but he really excelled in track. He was a swift and graceful runner and was part of his school's track team as well as a team in his Dorchester neighborhood. For several years, Danny had track meets or practices every single day after school and on Saturdays, too—he was so good, he collected a roomful of trophies for his speed. Since Danny's bro Brett was an equally good runner, their bedroom was bursting with track trophies!

Staying in top shape for track and his other sports was important to Danny, and it still is today. Although he hardly gets the time to play sports at all anymore, he's the New Kid who will seek out a nearby gym when the group's on the road and try to make time to work out. One look at his solid 'n sexy muscles and you can see he's doing a pretty good job of it!

It wasn't much of a stretch, as you can see, when Danny hit his teen years, to get into dancing. And did he ever—with a passion! From his athletic background, Danny was always a smooth and natural mover, and when the breakdancing craze hit Boston, Danny was first on the block with the most awesome of moves. "I picked it up," Danny says modestly, "just from being around, hanging out with friends and even watching TV." That may be so, but there's no question that Danny put his own unique spin on what he picked up—many feel that of all the New Kids, Danny Wood is the group's most natural and creative dancer. There's little question that when the group began, before they had a professional choreographer working with them, Danny was in the forefront, making up routines and teaching the other guys the steps.

His friend Donnie shared Danny's passion for breakdancing, though as a young teen Donnie was more into rapping. Together, the pair made up rap tunes and dynamic street steps to go with them. Danny can be a really dedicated hard worker when he puts his mind to something, and breakdancing, soul music and rap had captured his heart and soul to the max. He put almost every available minute into it!

Along with Donnie, and later Jordan Knight, Danny put his musical talents to work with the Dorchester Youth Collaborative, a youth organization through which he and his buddies put on breakdancing demonstrations all over Boston. They traveled around and put on shows for audiences mainly consisting of other teens who wanted to learn the technique. One summer Danny worked with Jordan teaching dancing to young kids at a day camp. Danny especially enjoyed working with the children. "I love kids," he says, and one day he plans to have a whole slew of his own.

During his teen years, Danny joined a group

called Rock Against Racism, with which he danced, rapped and put on shows as well. He was part of this group at the same time New Kids came along, and for one small moment, he wasn't sure he wanted to leave Rock Against Racism for New Kids.

Danny knew his share of tragedy as a teenager. It was during this time that he learned about death. For a couple of years in a row, or so it seemed to Danny, he lost many relatives, including an uncle, an aunt and his beloved grandfather, too. Since Danny was very close with his cousins who'd lost their parents, it hit him very hard. Danny found the losses and the sadness very difficult to deal with, but he surely learned something about the fragility of life and the value of family and following your heart.

Although he had an interest that kept him busy, Danny wasn't immune from the problems city kids, especially teenagers, are faced with. And his teen years weren't totally without incident. There was time spent hanging out on street corners with a wild crowd. "He's always been drawn to a wilder bunch of friends and liked to be where the action was," an old friend said, and Danny once let slip that he himself nearly got into some wrongdoing, but since he was underage at the time, he was let go with a stern warning. He didn't get into trouble again.

Danny's grown out of his street-life days with this philosophy: "If you're on the streets, you're looking for trouble. When I was on the streets, I'd always see people getting into trouble for drugs and whatnot. To me, being on the streets means you're not living up to your potential."

That point was brought home during a really scary incident that Danny has told reporters about. "I remember one time I was at a club in Boston and a whole bunch of fights were breaking out and carrying over to the street outside the club. I saw this guy I knew . . . well, I wasn't really friends with him or anything like that, but I had seen him around the neighborhood. And he just pulled out a gun and started shooting at this guy across the street who started shooting back at him. I crawled underneath a car and prayed that I'd get out alive! Everybody hit the ground. It was sick. After that, I never went to clubs much. It was just around that time I finally said to myself, 'Self, I've had enough. I've got to do something constructive with my life.'"

That Danny came to his senses is surely a testament to his strong and loving family background—and their emphasis on education. No matter how much hanging out Danny did, he was still expected to make good grades, and he did. After the Trotter School, Danny attended the Phyllis Wheatley Middle School (with Donnie) and then Copley High School in downtown Boston. Danny did best in subjects that inspired him; in high school it was U.S. History, where he made straight *A*s all the way through. Actually, he didn't do badly in his other subjects either, maintaining *A*s and *B*s in nearly all of them. If he had a weakness, it was in foreign languages.

In spite of Danny's fine academic record, he never seemed to have to work too hard at his studies—his mom always thought he could do better and that was the source of probably the only struggles Danny had with his parents. Until New Kids came along, that is.

When his best friend Donnie persuaded Danny to join the group, Danny knew right away it was something he wanted to do. But he, more than any other Kid, had terrible conflicts and difficult decisions to make. For one thing, he was involved in his Rock Against Racism group and didn't really want to give that up; he knew he wouldn't have time for both. But a much more pressing matter was that of school —and of his parents' wishes. Danny Wood had been bright enough in high school to qualify for a full four-year academic scholarship to one of the most prestigious colleges in the country, Boston University. Had he not gotten that scholarship, it's doubtful his family could have afforded to send him there. Naturally, his parents were thrilled. Education was always the highest priority for all their children; Danny would be the second Woods' child to be able to go to college on a scholarship.

Danny knew right away that he probably wasn't going to be able to give New Kids a full commitment—and that's what it required—*and* go to college at the same time. His parents were adamant that he accept the scholarship. It wasn't that they didn't want Danny to follow his heart into showbiz, only that they understood what an "iffy" thing showbiz is, that no matter how talented someone might be, no matter how hard they may try, there are no guarantees of ever making it. Danny's parents were skeptical about the group's chances. They pressed him to go to college instead.

For one semester Danny attempted to do both. He accepted that hard-to-get scholarship and attended classes during the day; he practiced with New Kids at night. But it wasn't working out. Danny's heart was with the group, not in the classroom. Although New Kids wasn't exactly taking off in those early days, Danny was getting deeper into not only the music and dreams of stardom but also the behind-the-scenes engineering, producing and writing end of it as well.

It was a dean at the college who, after all was

said and done, helped Danny make his decision.

Danny remembers, "The dean just said, 'Look, your heart is with the group and it could be a once-in-a-lifetime opportunity. Go with it; your scholarship will always be waiting for you if you want to come back. You're not going to lose it." Of course, that dean had to convince Danny's mother of the same thing before she gave her blessing to New Kids on the Block!

And it might surprise you to know that in spite of his New Kids success and their grueling schedule, Danny hasn't completely forgone his college education. He's taking some correspondence courses and getting credit for his on-the-road experiences, too. Who knows, one day he might even go back and get that degree.

4

Joseph McIntyre

BEING THE SOLE BLUE-EYED BABE OF THE BUNCH isn't the only thing that separates Joseph McIntyre from the other New Kids. For though little Joe and the guys feel like family *now,* he's the only one who didn't grow up in the Dorchester section of Boston and didn't know Donnie, Danny, Jon and Jordan before joining the group. In fact, Joe's upbringing, though not terribly far away from his New Kids buddies, was completely different.

He came into the world on the very last day of December in 1972—one last little "tax deduction" for his ecstatic parents—in a hospital in Needham, Massachusetts. Joe's folks, Thomas and Katherine, are deeply religious and immediately named their new blond bundle of joy Joseph, after St. Joseph. And in honor of a dear family friend whose surname was Mulrey, they gave the baby that as a middle name.

Of course, it wasn't as if Thomas and Kay (as Katherine McIntyre is usually called) had little practice in naming children—after all, they'd done it eight times previously! Joseph Mulrey McIntyre was the *ninth* (and last) child in the family. The role of "youngest," as he is in New Kids, is one that comes naturally to Joe.

In his own real-life family, he's preceded by seven sisters, Judith, Alice, Susan, Tricia, Carol, Jean and Kate, plus one big brother named Tommy. And, as you can imagine, right from the start, "Joe-Bird"—one among his many family nicknames—got used to being babied and never once complained about it!

It wasn't easy keeping up with a brood so large and busy as the McIntyres, but Thomas and Kay held a tight rein over the bunch. Thomas, a stout man with a head full of thick white hair, has been a bricklayer all his life and built many sturdy homes and condominiums in the Boston area. Today, he's vice-president of the bricklayers' union in Boston. Kay, too, works; she is a secretary for the Greater Boston Boy Scouts. But Kay McIntyre was always able to keep a steady eye on all her children; for one thing, her job wasn't very far from home; for another, she's never driven a car in her life, preferring to stay close to the nest and take buses when she has to get somewhere.

In fact, the McIntyre home, which Joe has lived in all his life, is just a stone's throw away from a bus station in the section of Boston called Jamaica Plain. It's not very far from Dorchester, or from Roxbury for that matter, where the other New Kids went to school, but never once did Joe's path cross those of Donnie, Danny, Jon and Jordan before they got together as New Kids. Joe's house, which he terms "fairly good sized," sits on top of a gently sloping hill on a dead-end street not very far from the serenity of a lovely park and pond. Growing up, Joe spent many an afternoon playing football in that very park with his friends.

The house itself has only two bathrooms but enough bedrooms so that Joe could have his own. Until recently, he slept in a bunk bed and lined his walls with his collection of baseball caps from every team in the USA. Now, of course, that hat collection must share space with all the gifts he's gotten from New Kids fans! Joe also has a TV in his room and a stereo. Before he got frantically busy with New Kids, he used to spend hours in his room listening to Michael Jackson records on that stereo. "I liked all kinds of Top 40 music," Joe relates. He was not particularly into rhythm 'n blues or rapping the way the other New Kids were, growing up just on the other side of town.

Instead, Joe was a small, dreamy kind of kid ("I'd always be daydreaming about what I wanted to do, instead of what I was doing!" he confesses) who wore braces and showed an early talent for art. Joe used to draw pictures all the time and some of his work is quite realistic and surprisingly good. There was a lot of laughter and good-natured teasing within his big family; Joe got along well with all his sisters and let off steam playfully roughhousing with his big brother Tommy, nearly four years his senior. Although he had so many big sisters to take care of him, Joe did learn to be somewhat independent: he can cook breakfast all by himself, just about anything you want.

Holidays, of course, were special times around the McIntyre household. Not only was the house filled with all eleven in the immediate family, but most often, relatives would come to visit and the house would be bursting at the seams. But that was okay with Joe and his siblings who fondly remember those holidays as the most fun times of the year. "We'd really get to goof off," Joe tattles, "pretending to be rock stars, jumping around and using tennis racquets as guitars." Joe's best Christmas ever was when he was only five years old and came down Christmas morning to find exactly what he'd wished for under the tree: "A Big Wheels tricycle with a siren on top! I loved it!" Joe acknowledges, of course, that these days Christmases are even more special to him: it's practically the only time of the year when all his family is reunited (three of his older sisters now live in different cities), and he can finally afford to buy really nice presents for *everyone.* In fact, with one of his first big paychecks, generous Joe bought his mother the plush coat she'd always wanted.

There is one aspect of Joe's growing-up years that *is* similar to that of his New Kids friends and that is the fact that church was very important to his family life. The McIntyre clan is devoutly Catholic, and going to church on Sundays was a sacred family tradition. Little Joe served as an altar boy for several years and he and his brother Tommy sang in the choir. That was not the kind of singing that Joe equated with pop stardom—we'll get to *that* in a moment!—but it was clear, even way back then, that Joseph Mulrey McIntyre had a beautiful singing voice.

Religion played such a big part in his family life that Joe's parents expressed worry when he joined New Kids on the Block and began traveling all over the country on tour. Joe's mom knew it wouldn't be easy, but she talked to her son seriously about attending Mass each week while he was on the road. "Just because you can sing doesn't make you any less a Catholic, or my son," she once said. Not just for his mom's wishes, but quietly and privately, Joe does try to keep up with his religious practices. While on stage he often wears the holy medallion he received for his confirmation. It features a rendering of the saint he was named for and on the back it says, "St. Joseph, pray for us." The only conflict Joe has had between being a New Kid and coming from a religious family is when his family is in the audience for a show and some of the fans' behavior embarrasses him. It's also been reported that his mom wasn't too thrilled with a bit of suggestiveness in one of the New Kids' videos. She even called the record company and voiced her displeasure. But, by and large, Joe is balancing his deep spirituality with his love of and commitment to New Kids—and New Kids fans—very well.

That he's been able to balance a spiritual life with a showbiz one shouldn't really be all that surprising, for in one way, Joe McIntyre has been preparing for stardom all his young life. In fact, of all the New Kids, he, the youngest, is the one who came to the band with the most performing experience.

Performing has always been a McIntyre "family affair," and, no doubt, along with their religion, it's a shared joy that's helped keep the family ties strong. It all started because Mom Kay, always a performer at heart, joined up with a local community theater group, singing and acting in many small-scale productions. While not *all* nine McIntyre children loved the stage equally well, three of the girls, Judith, Susan and Carol, got right into it. Judith, in fact, is today a professional actress who lives and works in New York City. But, as it turned out, no one took to performing more than the littlest of the crew, Joseph Mulrey! Although he never had a formal lesson, he began singing at the age of five and added acting to his credits a year later. Joe joined the Neighborhood Children's Theater of Boston and, along with sixty or seventy other youngsters, put on musicals such as *Oliver* and *The Music Man,* plus straight dramatic productions such as *Our Town.* They performed during weekends and holiday seasons all over the community. Joe began to perform in other local community theaters as well, and although *he* doesn't consider himself a "ham," he realized early that he felt quite at ease in the spotlight. In fact, for Joe, the performing part of being a New Kid has always been his very favorite. That's why he seems so natural up on stage; he's lovin' every minute of it!

Joe looks back on his days performing in community theater fondly. His best memory is the time the entire family was in a play together. "We all got to sing and act and my dad was sitting in the back row of the auditorium and was so proud to see us all together. It was great!" By the time New Kids came along, the McIntyre clan was beginning to earn a bit of a showbiz reputation of their own, at least in the neighborhood, anyway.

Unlike the other New Kids, Joe did not attend public school, neither in his Jamaica Plain neighborhood nor by being bused to an inner-city school. Instead, Joe followed his sisters and brother into the parochial school system and attended St. Marys from kindergarten until high school. There, he wore a regulation school uniform and was taught by nuns. Although the little blond boy sometimes spoke out of turn in school, he was never disruptive or a discipline problem. Joe was a good student who excelled in math, English and writing.

It was in parochial school that Joe made most of his friends, and those are the kids he counts as his true confidants today. Like the other New Kids, it's hard for Joe to know whether people he meets now want to be pals because they like *him* or because he's famous. With his old friends, he doesn't have to worry. Back in the days before New Kids, Joe spent many a happy after-school hour tossing a football back and forth with his buddies or playing basketball or even doing homework together. Nowadays, on his rare time off, he's likely to try and scare up a racquetball game with his old friends or perhaps a round of golf, Joe's newest sporting passion.

His friends will tell you that Joe hasn't changed a whole lot since the band took off— of course, he's grown much taller and gotten a lot more savvy, but Joe is still the same funny, charming, peaceful guy he always was. He's still a bit of a wise guy but as friendly, open and down to earth as ever before. He hasn't turned into a big shot and he hasn't turned his back on his old friends.

By the time Joe entered Catholic Memorial High School, he was already part of New Kids. It's easy to forget that Joe joined in 1985, before his thirteenth birthday, and with the other Kids worked hard for several *years* before *Hangin' Tough* brought them the fame they deserved. So all of Joe's junior high and high school years were spent as a member of the band—he was the one who always had a full load of homework in addition to learning all the New Kids songs, dance routines, recordings and performances. Still, Joe managed to get exemplary grades in high school. His biggest disappointment, in fact, was when the band really took off, and because he had to work with a tutor on the road, he didn't make the honor roll for the first time in his high school career.

NEW KIDS ON THE BLOCK

arry Busacca / RETNA LTD.

NEW KIDS ON THE BLOCK are *(left to right)* Danny Wood, Donnie Wahlberg, Joe McIntyre and Jordan and Jon Knight.

Todd Kaplan / STAR FILE

Except for Joe *(center)*, Jon, Jordan, Donnie and Danny attended the same school and played ball together on the streets of Boston. Now they perform on a different stage—but they're still "Hangin' Tough."

Steve Granitz / RETNA LTD.

Individual flair and the hot mix of rap, song, and dance have made NEW KIDS a sensational pop phenomenon; but they never lose their cool.

Posing backstage at the 17th annual American Music Awards, the NEW KIDS were all smiles after winning awards for ''Hangin' Tough,'' favorite pop-rock album, and favorite pop-rock group.

You can bet the girls scream when Danny sings "I Need You."

Larry Busacca / RETNA LTD.

Tough-guy Donnie sings "Cover Girl" to a lucky member of the audience.

Joe, the youngest KID, takes time out to call someone special.

Vinnie Zuffante / STAR FILE

Brothers—adorable Jon and sexy Jordan— were on hand to celebrate fellow chart- topper Tiffany's 18th birthday in L.A.

Whether on stage . . .

or just hangin' out—from their hometown of Boston to as far away as Japan—NEW KIDS are a *smash hit!*

They've got . . .

Photos by David Seelig / STAR FILE

"The Right Stuff."

Donnie raps with the crowd on "Hangin' Tough."

Irresistible Joe breaks hearts whenever he sings "Please Don't Go Girl."

◁

◆

○

Jordan takes lead on "I'll Be Loving You (Forever)."

Their smiles tell it all: these guys *love* to perform!

Dressed to kill at the Grammy Living Legends special in November 1989, NEW KIDS performed a medley of Smokey Robinson's hits in tribute to the Motown legend.

Danny

Joe

**NEW KIDS
ON
THE BLOCK**

Jordan

Vinnie Zuffante / STAR FILE

Donnie

Jeffrey Kane / RETNA LTD.

7

Jon

Vinnie Zuffante / STAR FILE

Jon will never forget
the very first time he
heard a NEW KIDS
song on the radio.

NEW KIDS ON THE BLOCK

Backstage before a show, the KIDS always psych themselves up so they can hit the stage and give the best performance possible.

"Are you ready to rock?!"

The NEW KIDS ON THE BLOCK are . . . for a long, long time.

But that wasn't his biggest problem as the youngest member of New Kids. When he joined, in June of 1985, the core of the group, Donnie, Danny, Jon and Jordan, was already in place. Not only did they all know each other but Joe was brought in to replace a good friend of Donnie's, a neighborhood boy named Jamie Kelly whose parents did not want him in showbiz.

Joe McIntyre was specifically recruited by New Kids producer Maurice Starr, who went looking for a boy who was younger than the others, with a sweet, high-pitched voice. The idea was to create a group similar to the Osmonds of the '70s—and they wanted a Kid who could not only hit those high notes but who could also conceivably be a teen idol as well. Everyone in the group understood the concept when Joe was brought aboard, but that didn't make it any easier for them to accept him right off. For one thing, they couldn't help being slightly resentful of the boy who took their friend's place—that's just human nature. For another, the other four recognized right away that Joe was not from their neighborhood and thought he might be a little square. They admit that they picked on Joe in those early days, really gave him a hard time.

It's a testament to Joe's strong will and love of performing that he stuck with it all. For not only did he feel unwelcome at first, it was also hard being two years younger than the next youngest member (Jordan) and lots smaller, too. When the band first got together, Joe was not even five feet tall and barely tipped the scales at ninety pounds! Add to that the burden of a full schedule of classes and homework, and you can see that the littlest New Kid had the most to overcome.

Joe always had the wholehearted support of his family, however, who encouraged him to continue with the band. And it didn't take very long at all before Joe wormed his way into the hearts of all the guys in the group and was made to feel just like family. Now, they can all barely remember feeling any other way toward him!

Joe is seventeen now and has certainly come a long way from when New Kids first began. He's just about finished with high school and is even thinking about taking college courses in music and in English. Although he plans on staying on top with New Kids for a long, long time, in the back of his creative Kid's head is the idea that maybe someday he'll be a journalist or even write a book. Surely, his experiences with New Kids would be the perfect way to start!

5

New Kids Love Stories

THEY DON'T CALL THEM "THE HARDEST-WORKING kids in showbiz" for nothing. In the past two years, New Kids on the Block have been on a nonstop whirlwind schedule of rehearsing, recording, touring, appearing on television and doing personal and charitable performances as well. That's not to mention learning new material and even creating new music of their own! That kind of hectic schedule would knock the wind out of even the most energetic young go-getter.

Where does that leave time, or energy, for a private life—or better yet, for a love life? No surprise, it really doesn't! Having a girlfriend is harder now for Donnie, Danny, Jon, Jordan and Joe than at any other time in their lives, but that doesn't mean they don't think about girls. In this chapter, you'll uncover each boy's heart secrets and find out how each one really feels about girls, fans, love and romance.

DONNIE
"I've Lost in Love"

Donnie Wahlberg has never been uncomfortable around girls—after all, he grew up with four older sisters who took turns doting on him. Donnie grooved on the attention; it's one of the reasons he got into showbiz in the first place. Even when he was just rapping on the streets of Boston with his posse, for him the main attraction was "hearing the girls screaming!"

It's no surprise that, as a kid, outgoing charmer Donnie was very popular and, much to his parents' chagrin, began dating early—and often! He didn't have a serious girlfriend until he was sixteen, but that experience almost made him never want to fall in love again.

"My first love was a great learning experience for me," Donnie confessed to a teen magazine. "It taught me a lot. I was in love with a girl and then she left me for another guy."

Seems the young lady in question had been seeing someone who moved away. She thought it was over; the other guy didn't, and one day he came back for her. Donnie's girl went back to her old flame. "She took me for granted," Donnie remembers. "She figured I'd always be there, waiting for her. And you know what, I was!" Foolishly, Donnie gave this girl another chance, only to have her leave him again.

After that experience, Donnie went through a period of being very careful about getting too involved emotionally. He protected his heart against hurt by becoming a real flirt. "I was always winking or waving at the girls," he relates, "letting them know that I was very available." But if he found himself falling for one girl, Donnie quickly pulled back and found another girl to flirt with.

Happily, those days are just about over and Donnie is starting to remember how great it was to be in love. When he's asked—and he's always asked!—what kind of girl he goes for, Donnie usually comes up with some clever quip about wanting someone "cute, intelligent and not after my money." But way down deep inside, the real Donnie holds loyalty and trustworthiness above all other qualities. And this: "Someone I can be comfortable with who doesn't judge me or treat me differently because of who I am. I think everyone should be treated the same whether they're famous or not. People are people."

He sees that it's really hard now, when he meets someone, to know if she's interested because he's a star, or if she'd like him anyway. "I can meet a girl tomorrow," he explains, "who four years ago would not give me the time of day. Now, she's all ready to marry me. I don't want that. I want someone who loves me for me! It might take ten years to find someone who does not know who I am and who cares about me and loves me and I love them. I'll wait until the time is right."

Of course, there's a part of Donnie that hopes he doesn't have to wait *too* long, for as he remembers it, "The feeling of being in love is great. And any girl who wins my love, I can promise her she'll be the happiest girl in the world. When I'm in love, I'm in love and I will do anything for a girl I love."

JON
The Love Story No One's Supposed to Know About

He's known as the shyest New Kid and he is, except when it comes to girls, that is. Jonathan Knight has never been shy about letting his feelings be known and has *always* had his eye on the opposite sex. He had his first crush when he was only eight years old. "I don't remember her name," he muses, "but she was small and cute. I used to walk her home from school—she lived right next door to the school." In sixth grade, Jon and Donnie actually had a crush on the same red-haired girl, though neither boy actually did anything about it.

Jon started dating at an early age and always had great success—he admits to having been in love and says he hasn't had his heart broken yet. In fact, though no one's supposed to know about it, Jonathan Knight is in love right now! The object of his affection? Pop star Tiffany.

They met two years ago when New Kids hopped on tour as Tiffany's opening act. At the time, she was much better known than they were and very gracious about giving the New Kids a chance with her audience. As they toured the country together, naturally Tiffany and all the New Kids got to know each other pretty well. The boys were all drawn to her naturalness and friendliness and she ended up liking all of them, especially the oldest Kid, Jon Knight. It seemed the two of them had the most in common and could really talk easily to each other. Both were from broken homes and both cherished quiet moments. It didn't take very long before those warm feelings turned to love.

And *that* presented problems. For one thing,

their tandem tour couldn't last forever, and it was inevitable, with their burgeoning careers, that Jon and Tiffany would have to separate. She had other tour commitments; he had albums to record and more concerts to do, this time with New Kids as headliners. Jon made no bones about the fact that the separation was difficult. "It's a strain because it's like a long-distance relationship. It's rough when you don't see someone for months. The only way to communicate is to talk on the phone."

But that wasn't the worst of their problems, and it, in fact, turned out to be pretty solvable when Tiffany signed up with New Kids management. They see each other all the time now. No, the other problem was of a more delicate nature. Simply put, both Tiffany and Jon were seemingly advised to keep the true nature of their relationship under wraps. They've been told to tell the press that they're "just friends" and to try and avoid being photographed together.

Good kids Jon and Tiffany haven't balked at the advice from the pros who handle their careers. Whether they agreed or not, they have tried to be cooperative. That hasn't stopped other New Kids from spilling the beans to reporters, though. Little Joe McIntyre admitted it to an American magazine over a year ago and just recently babbled to the British press about Jon and Tiff. And anyone who sees the two of them together knows it's true: They're head over heels in love. In fact, the whisperings *now* have the lovebirds talking about getting engaged.

Will they? Will their relationship, after all, weather the test of time and the incredible pressures of their hot careers? Stay tuned!

JORDAN
Is He Afraid of Falling in Love?

Gorgeous Jordan Knight never had a problem wondering whether girls liked him or not—from the time he was little, they stuck to him like jelly to peanut butter! The only problem was that little Jordan wasn't much interested in returning the attention. As a kid, anyway, Jordan just seemed to have other things on his mind, whether it was reading his books, playing his keyboards, or singing in church choir. He was not precocious with girls.

He didn't have his first crush until he was thirteen. "The girl's name was Pam and it was crazy," he recalls. "She blew my mind. I never kissed before. I didn't know how to. We worked it out." The fate of Jordan's first crush, however, left *him* crushed and *may* have affected his feelings about falling in love ever again. "She left me," Jordan confesses. "She went to summer camp and met another guy."

Ever since that time, Jordan's been very cautious about dating and getting involved with any one girl. He's never understood why girls consider him good-looking. Modest Jordan sees himself as rather average-looking, "Just kind of a guy-next-door type."

Even though he'd be loath to make a commitment, still Jordan can't deny that he's definitely attracted to girls. Here's his description of someone he could, at least, *like!* "She's gotta be nice, funny, charming, witty and independent. And she can't let other people tell her what to do."

Jordan understands that even if he *were* looking for love, it would be pretty impossible at this stage of his New Kids career. "We're always on the road and I wouldn't even think about starting a relationship on the road, you can't put any time into it. So for now, we just look!"

DANNY
A Secret Girlfriend?

Danny Wood's never been the easiest New Kid to figure out. Quiet and sometimes mysterious, it's hard to know what's really on his mind. And when it comes to girls, and the question of whether he has a special friend or not, Danny boy has given conflicting accounts!

He does admit to having his first crush back when he was only five years old. "The girl's name was Beth and she had a bowl haircut. That's all I remember—I never had the nerve to say anything to her!"

He found the nerve with other girls later on, however, and began to date in junior high school. His mom laughingly remembers Danny having many, many girlfriends. "I couldn't keep up with who the girlfriend was this week, it kept changing." Danny did have a steady when he was about sixteen, and more recently, he's slyly referred to someone back in Boston, keeping the home fires burning. To most reporters he answers that he doesn't have a girlfriend, but once he opened up and admitted, "I have a girlfriend at home. It's hard; I've been with her for about a year. I'd been doing this [New Kids] for three years before I met her and she knows that this is very important to me; she understands."

Whether this is a serious relationship or not, only Danny and this girl know, but he *is* candid about enjoying the attention from New Kids female fans. He loves meeting girls, and as long as "They approach me nice and quietly, and don't rip my clothing or anything," he wouldn't rule out even going on a date with a fan. Danny feels most comfortable with "a girl I can tell anything to." Is that the girl back home?

JOE
A Newcomer to Love

Joe McIntyre *should* be very comfortable around girls, coming from a home with seven sisters—and he is. "Joe's the ladies' man in the group, the real flirt," the other Kids have tattled. But what they don't say is that, in reality, Joe's the one with the least experience in that department. After all, he joined the band at twelve years old and has been so busy between New Kids and school, he never really had much chance to develop a social life. When New Kids hit and Joe hit the road with them, he'd never had a true girlfriend, never really been on an official date!

He does remember a crush he had when he was twelve years old, however. "We were both in the Neighborhood Children's Theater, and because all my friends were always flirting with the girls, I kind of got hooked up with her. Her name was Chrissie and we sort of liked each other for six months or so. The first time she broke it off, I cried. Then the second time, I broke it off."

Being new to the dating-and-love game is sometimes weird for Joe. He doesn't see himself—or anyone in the band, for that matter—as much of a sex symbol. He doesn't even think he's much to look at! "Girls say I'm cute," he bashfully acknowledges. "*I* don't think I'm cute. I don't know why they do . . . must be my big feet!"

Hanging around with Donnie, Danny, Jon and Jordan, however, has rubbed off on Joe somewhat. He's certainly had time to rap with the other guys and decide what kind of girl catches his eye. "Independence, good looks and charm are important to me, but a great sense of humor is the main quality that turns me on. A girl with goals of her own, who doesn't live her life through me, now that's what I'd like."

In one way it's even harder for Joe than it is for the other guys who've had girlfriends before to know if a girl's after him just because he's famous. "It would be nice," he thinks, "to find a girl who'd say, 'I really didn't know too much about New Kids on the Block but when I went to the concert, I learned a lot about them and I liked you. You guys put on a good show' . . . stuff like that."

As for the taunts of his bandmates that he's really the New Kid to watch out for, Joe laughingly responds, "I love girls. I wouldn't say I'm a heartbreaker. I like to flirt, but it's innocent!"

6

Which Kid Is for You?

SURE, YOU LOVE THEM *ALL*, BUT WHICH KID'S personality is the best match for *yours?* Which Kid do you have the most in common with? Which Kid would you have the best chance with, once you finally *do* meet face-to-face? In this chapter, you'll find out what each Kid is really like and what his idea of a great date would be. One thing to know right up front: All five of them say they *would* date one of their fans.

DONNIE WAHLBERG

Born: August 17, 1969
Age: 20
Vital Statistics: 5'10" tall, 155 lbs., blond hair and hazel eyes.

He's the original New Kid—and if there's one thing about Donnie, he's a total original in every sense! Donnie describes himself as "unpredictable, wild and crazy," and there's a side to him that very much fits that description. He's the New Kids' streetwise babe who's overflowing with energy—he's always on the go—and very changeable. Once you think you've got him pegged, he turns around and says or does something that's completely the opposite. Donnie's style can change from day to day!

Donnie's definitely got a rough edge; although he's young, he's seen a lot in his life and has some very definite and strong opinions. He's not always careful about what he says, especially if he feels someone's "dissin'" the band or someone he loves. That's how Donnie talks: "Dissin'" is a streetwise term for being disrespectful, and it's one of the things Donnie tolerates least. "I'm the one who's always ready to speak up," Donnie admits. "I'm the one who always wants to get revenge!" He's outspoken, impulsive and always ready for anything.

73

But there's another side to daring Donnie as well, the "caring, lovable" guy who's outgoing, very sociable and a real charmer. He never misses an opportunity to give a compliment—and you know that he's sincere. He's generous and gets a kick out of gift-giving; last year Donnie surprised his mom with a brand-new home and is looking forward to buying one for his dad soon.

The girl for Donnie would have to pay him a bucketload of attention; he admits he really thrives on it. She'd have to have a great sense of humor, be honest and trustworthy, too. And of course, she'd have to be impulsive and understanding of his hectic schedule.

Looks don't mean a whole lot to him. To Donnie, it's what's inside a person that counts, not what they look like. "I go for girls of all races, shapes and sizes," he's said. Even though he's "intense about girls, whether I'm meeting a new one or going on a date or just having fun," Donnie's been very careful about giving his heart away to just one. Right now, he'd be the New Kid to want to date lots of different girls rather than settling in with one. So if it's a commitment you're after, Donnie's probably not your guy.

On the other hand, if you're up for an unpredictable fun time on a date, it's Donnie who'll show it to you. He's a take-charge kind of guy, so he'd be the one to plan your time together; it could be a movie, dancing or a ride around town in his Jeep, but it would definitely include getting something to eat. Donnie's the New Kid with the healthiest appetite; he loves to eat! But that doesn't necessarily mean going to an expensive restaurant—Donnie's just as happy with a local fast-food fried-chicken place or a couple of slices of pizza than anything more formal. A date with Donnie would no doubt include lots of laughter and, very possibly, lots of other people as well. Party-animal Donnie likes the company of others, especially when he gets the chance to hang out with people who aren't connected with showbiz.

Knowing Donnie involves understanding something else—his serious side. The thing that's most important to him in the whole world is peace. Wearing peace medallions and using the phrase "Peace Out," which he does a lot, are not just trendy things for him. Donnie deeply believes in peace, among people and among all the countries of the world.

He's a complicated and unusual mix, that Donnie W., he can be tough; he's outgoing and gregarious; but he's also tender and peace-loving. He doesn't hide any of the sides of his personality—with Donnie, "what you see is what you get." And that's what makes him so irresistible!

JONATHAN KNIGHT
Birthday: November 29, 1968
Age: 21
Vital Statistics: 5'11" tall, 155 lbs., brown hair, hazel eyes

Call him Jonathan. That's the first thing to know about this dark 'n dreamy babe, for that's really what he prefers to be called by the people closest to him. And once you get to know Jonathan, there's little doubt you're going to want to be one of those people.

Jonathan's known as the shyest Kid and in some respects that's true. He doesn't seek the spotlight; he hasn't always wanted to be the center of attention. But Jonathan's not shy when it comes to approaching and talking to girls. He's soft-spoken, has no qualms about coming right up to a girl and introducing himself. He's very much a gentleman—Jon's the guy who'd carry your books or stoop to pick something up if you dropped it—and he's got the greatest knack for making even the most ill-at-ease person feel comfortable. That's partly because Jonathan's a great listener. Coming from such a diverse family, he learned to really listen to other people, and frankly, he simply and honestly cares about what you have to say.

Jon's sensitive. He admits to being "the group worrier," and perhaps because he's the senior member of the band, he feels a lot of responsibility toward his younger brother Jordan and all the guys. "Jon's always the one worried about our schedule, worried about all the little details of touring and traveling and the show. He's very efficient and likes things to go smoothly," the other guys say about him. Jon himself feels that. "I always looked after my brother, Jordan. He's the kind of guy that's so easygoing, things go right by him. Now, I kinda look out for the whole group." If you like your guys big-brotherly, that's Jon!

There's also something of the loner in Jon Knight. If there's one New Kid likely to be apart from the pack, nine times out of ten, it's him. It's not because Jon doesn't love being with his New Kids buddies, but he's the type who really does need time alone sometimes, just to wander around in a new environment, just to think and enjoy some solitude.

Jon isn't very good at hiding his feelings, he's not "macho"; he even admits to tears once in a while when things really move him.

Jonathan likes people with all different kinds of personalities. In fact, he claims that he doesn't dislike *anyone,* he gets along with everyone! Generally, though, he goes for girls who are "nice, who let their real personalities shine through, and who don't treat me any differently because of being in New Kids on the Block." Upon further reflection, he adds,

"I'd go for somebody sweet, someone I can talk to, someone who understands me and is independent."

Efficient Jon is a planner, so a date with him would be well thought out; he's not terribly impulsive. Although he enjoys movies and restaurants, he'd be just as happy to have you over to his place where he'd cook a great Italian dinner. Parties and dance clubs are not for him; quiet evenings spent talking and listening to music are definitely more this good-natured Kid's style.

Right now, of course, Jon's kind of unavailable, but who knows what the future will bring? If you do get the chance to meet this handsome, self-effacing dreamer, approach him quietly and gently. Jon will know you're interested in him as a person, if you keep the conversation cool and away from gossipy, giggly questions. And there's no question that meeting and getting to know Jon is well worth your while!

JORDAN KNIGHT
Birthday: May 17, 1970
Age: Nearly 20
Vital Statistics: 5'10" tall, 155 lbs., brown hair, brown eyes

There are two Jordan Knights. One is the most outgoing, affectionate charmer you've ever laid eyes on. This is the Jordan who's really laid-back, who hardly ever worries, who sincerely likes people and likes to have a good time. This Jordan is unselfish, undemanding and *always* looks on the bright side of any situation: There are no dark clouds marring his view of life!

Baby-of-the-family Jordan has enjoyed being pampered to some degree and can even be a bit spacy when it comes to nitty-gritty details. He's a happy-go-lucky dude who often opts to "go with the flow."

But there's another side to Jordan Knight as well. He's the one, all the New Kids admit, who is the most creative musically. "Jordan's very into his music, not just singing with the New Kids, but working on his keyboards, composing new tunes, writing new lyrics," they agree. Jordan's always been into the creative part of making music, and there's no question that with or without New Kids, music was always going to be a part of his life. It's Jordan who'll most often seek out other bands, who'll come up with new musical ideas for their act, who's interested in the technical end of studio work, who'll one day have a major hand in what material goes on to the New Kids' LPs.

This Jordan is not outspoken but more the smooth, silent leader type, especially when it comes to New Kids' direction.

When it comes to girls, *both* Jordans are certainly loving and caring. But the creative Jordan might need to spend more time alone, working on his music in solitude, than making the dating scene! He knows what he likes: "Girls who are charming, like to have fun and are romantic," and there's little doubt that if Jordan *did* fall for someone, he could fall hard. "When I get into something, whether it's music, or a romance, I get into it completely," he's revealed. "I'm emotional and like girls who aren't afraid to show their feelings either."

A date with Jordan would certainly be a special experience—what it probably wouldn't be is planned! Jordan's laid-back attitude certainly extends to his dating life, but things he likes to do range from a night on the town at the hottest dance club to an evening on a secluded beach by a roaring fire. Jordan may not be the best planner, but there's a romantic streak in him a mile wide!

What should you do if you spy Jordan and want to meet him? First of all, it would be up to you—Jordan's actually shy about approaching girls! But you should definitely go up to New Kids' handsome lead-singer heart-throb in a calm and collected way and just say "Hi." After all, Jordan reminds you, "I'm a normal person, and I would really like to meet you!"

DANNY WOOD
Birthday: May 14, 1969
Age: Almost 21
Vital Statistics: 5'7" tall, 145 lbs., black hair, brown eyes

Dimpled Danny describes himself as "nice, lovable, and laid-back," but also, "stubborn, someone who needs to be cared for." Indeed, New Kids' freshest dancer is a bit of all those things. He can be easygoing and is certainly one of the nicest guys you'll meet, but once Danny makes a decision about something, you'll have a tough time changing his mind!

While he's not the quietest New Kid—that title belongs to Jon!—Danny's not the most talkative either (by now you know that Donnie is!). He's more the strong, silent type who's got a real sensitive soul underneath. Danny has the ability to make the people around him feel comfortable, and no matter how famous or rich he becomes, he could never be a snob. Danny would never forget his roots and he truly believes that being a New Kid doesn't make him better than anyone else.

Still, being in the band is one of the most important things in his life, not because it's made him a star but because loyal Danny thinks of the group as family, and he'd go anywhere or do anything to defend his family and keep it together. "He's the most group-oriented guy in the band," his best friend Donnie once said. "He's like the link that keeps us all together." Danny's also the guy the others go to when they need a shoulder to lean on or a sympathetic ear. "He's always there with a smile," says Donnie, "to pick you up when you're down."

Pinning Danny down to a specific personality type is tough—he can go from conservative to crazy, and though he's really very grounded, he does have a bit of a wild streak in him, too!

Danny's very definite about the kind of girls he goes for. A girl's eyes are the first thing he notices: he thinks you can tell a lot about a girl by looking in her eyes. He also admits to a fondness for long hair. But more important than looks is personality, and having a sense of humor is his number-one requirement in that department. Even more crucial, however, is a girl's attitude. Danny would not consider even being friends with a girl if she weren't "completely tolerant of all kinds of people." Danny himself has grown up and benefited from being friends with people of all backgrounds, and he'd never pick a girl who was narrow-minded or prejudiced in any way.

Staying in shape is more important to this New Kid than to the others. He puts a high premium on being athletic and really enjoys going to the gym and working out. A girl who felt the same way would most definitely have a head start with this gorgeous Kid. In fact, Danny's idea of a great date would be to meet at the gym and exercise side-by-side. He loves the outdoors, so doing anything like bike riding, playing ball, even going for a run on the beach would be his idea of a perfect day.

As for nighttime activities, there's a whole range of things Danny likes to do. Going out to a dinner of Chinese or Italian food and topping the evening off at a dance club would suit him just fine, but then again, so would staying home (he'd cook) and just "chillin'" by the fireplace. Taking a special girl for a long walk by the river would be fulfilling, too.

Danny's a serious dude who says he likes to be taken care of. What he means by that is not someone waiting on him but someone understanding of the great demands on his time. He's definitely not the type to go out with several different girls at once. He's very much a one-girl guy who dreams of being married and having a family someday. "Being on the road so much has taught me how hectic and crazy life can be," Danny reveals. "I really see the value of settling down one day." There's no end to the girls who'd like to take him up on that!

JOE McINTYRE
Birthday: December 31, 1972
Age: 17
Vital Statistics: 5'7", 135 lbs., brown hair, blue
eyes

Sweet 'n innocent Joe McIntyre is the kind of guy anyone could fall for. He's completely guileless, friendly and outgoing. Joe sincerely likes people, and it shows. The youngest New Kid says about himself, "I'm chilled out, y'know? Fun. I think I have a good sense of humor. I'm not sensitive, but sentimental. Family-oriented." That's how Joe talks!

He's from a bit more sheltered background than the other New Kids and is just discovering people and the world. It's Joe's natural personality to be cautious and conservative. He doesn't make snap judgments about anyone or anything. He takes his time with decisions, but once he makes them, he usually sticks by them.

Joe's not one to be off by himself or seeking solitude; he's the guy who's ready to jump into any conversation with a joke or any argument with an opinion. He says he's "hyperactive," but, really, he's just majorly energetic!

Because Joe has such a sunny, sweet personality, a side of him that most people don't get to see is his hardworking side. When Joe takes on a new challenge—be it a dance step or learning to play the guitar—he gives it his *all*. He doesn't get distracted or thrown off track easily; until he masters something new, he's totally focused on it. That's one of the reasons he stuck with New Kids in the very beginning, when he was the "outsider" and the other Kids knew each other *and* all the material already. Joe just put his mind to being accepted and fitting in—and wouldn't you know it, he did just that in a very short time!

As you know, Joe doesn't have a whole lot of dating experience, but he *is* drawn to girls who are more independent than dependent, who have interests and goals of their own, apart from an interest in him. Joe likes to talk to girls about things like the New Kids' show or about music, movies, TV or just about anything. The only thing that makes him uncomfortable is when a girl gets gushy—"Please don't run up to me and say 'I love you,'" Joe cautions. "It makes me feel weird." Although Joe likes almost everyone he's met so far, he gets turned off right away by people who lie or are deceitful in any way. And if he figures out that someone's hanging out just to be "seen" with him, that's a total turn-off to this talented babe.

Spending a day with Joe might include a round of golf, his favorite sport. But if you didn't know how to play at all, miniature golf would be just fine with him, too. Window-shopping at a mall seems like a real ordinary thing to do, but for Joe, who doesn't get to do it too often, it would be a treat. Of course, he *does* have a problem with being recognized in those situations. He'd probably wear one of his trademark hats and hope for the best.

Nighttime fun would be a movie, especially a comedy, or even a dance club for a few hours. But what Joe would really love would be the chance to get to know his date. "Going for dinner and then a walk, just the two of us," he dreams.

Joe certainly plans on marriage and children, but that's a long way off. He's got a lot of life to experience before that; why, he hasn't even had his very first real girlfriend yet. But he is definitely looking!

7

All That
Secret Stuff

How much do you really know about New Kids on the Block? Test yourself and see how many of these 100 plus secrets you knew!

MUSICAL SECRETS

Many of their hit songs have a fresh new spin on them, but the truth is they were written five, ten, even fifteen years ago! "Please Don't Go Girl," their first big hit, was written twenty years ago when producer Maurice Starr was a teenager!

Their first album, *New Kids on the Block,* was really just "an experimental project."

Nevertheless, it took them one and a half

years to record it! (So much for being an "overnight sensation.")

Do you remember what the first single from that first LP was? It was called "Be My Girl," and it was released back in April '86. It flopped, along with that whole first album.

They got their name from a rap tune on that first album, called, of course, "New Kids on the Block." That rap was written by Donnie!

By their second album, *Hangin' Tough,* they had it together, but did you know that Danny Wood engineered most of it?

Hangin' Tough, the album, sold more copies in December '89 than any other record that month. All told, it's sold over seven million copies in the USA alone!

Hangin' Tough has a message: "Don't let anybody get in the way of what you want to do. Go out and do it, hang tough."

Jordan sang lead on "I'll Be Lovin' You (Forever)," the third single from *Hangin' Tough.*

The video for "(You Got It) The Right Stuff" was filmed in Louisiana in the fall of 1988.

All the tracks for their *Merry, Merry Christmas* album were recorded while they were on the road, in various hotel rooms.

Jon Knight, rarely a lead singer, took front-'n-center position on "Chestnuts Roasting on an Open Fire" and "White Christmas."

Donnie couldn't get just the right raspy tone in his voice for the lead on "Last Night I Saw Santa Claus," so producer Maurice Starr woke him from a sound sleep and told him to record it right then. Donnie's deep, raspy "morning" voice came out just perfectly!

Most of their fourth album, *Step by Step,* was also recorded in various hotel rooms all over the country while NKOTB was on the road.

Maurice Starr decides who sings lead on each song he comes up with. Usually, he tries Jordan first for the songs, especially those needing a high tenor in the lead. Then he'll try Jon on lead, or Donnie, Joe or Danny to see whose voice works best for each song.

New Kids plan to keep on experimenting with their style so they can grow musically, but they totally rule out ever coming out with a heavy-metal record.

CONCERT SECRETS

The first-ever show they did was at a prison on Deer Island, Massachusetts.

Whether it was from stage fright, or the audience, Jon admits his knees shook during that entire premiere performance!

Jordan was so petrified that first time out that when his lead parts came up, he wouldn't go to the front of the stage. He stood in back and hid behind his microphone.

When they first began to really hit the concert trail, they would sing while a prerecorded backup track played in the background. Now, they have a live band playing for them. Soon, they plan to play their own instruments.

Once, in the "bad old days," they were actually booed off the stage. Maybe the audience didn't like their outfits: They all used to dress alike, in silver and gold shiny shirts.

One time, way back then, a shaky stage collapsed on them!

Another time, Jordan fell into the audience.

Nowadays, they've gotten so comfortable on stage, they often improvise, so no two shows are exactly the same.

All the Kids have a lot of input into their live shows. It was Jon's idea (after seeing Debbie Gibson do it) to add lasers and pyrotechnics to their gigs; it was Donnie's and Jordan's idea to add the entire Christmas segment to the concerts they did around the holidays.

Even *they* don't always know where and when they're playing. That's because new shows keep being added to the tour to satisfy the demand!

The Kids' moms and their families often attend their shows. Altogether, there are thirty family members; the fans have dubbed them "The Posse 30."

On the last tour, Donnie wanted to be able to jump over the drum set at the end of the show; Jordan wanted to construct a contraption that would let the boys swing out over the audience. Neither idea was workable, so they settled for having a catwalk built above the stage that let them come out for an encore in a totally original way.

DONNIE SECRETS

He hoards things, never throws anything away.

He's very messy!

As a high school student, he studied the Chinese language for a while.

He loves to shop for clothes, especially on trendy Newberry Street in Boston.

During New Kids' early years ('84–'88), he went to school, had a part-time job at a bank *and* rehearsed every single day with the band.

He finished high school with a tutor.

He used to collect little figures of army men.

He has a stepbrother named Jeremy who lives in California. They only recently met.

He's left-handed.

Donnie calls his older brother Robert "Bobbo"; Bobbo calls *him* "Dinkydonno."

Donnie loves roller coasters but hates ferris wheels.

His ankles sometimes get sore from all that jumping around the stage he does.

When he's home, his favorite thing to do is pick up his old friend Jay, jump in his Jeep and drive around Boston.

"Peace Out" is Donnie's favorite expression.

No matter if he's wearing an old T-shirt and ripped jeans, or some fancy threads for a photo shoot or concert, Donnie's *never* without his peace medallion.

He idolizes . . . Cookie Monster, from "Sesame Street." "We have the same personality," he jokes. "Loud and attention-seeking. Plus we both have big feet."

Donnie says his worst trait is "impatience."

He's producing a rap group called The Northside Posse; they're friends from high school.

Sometimes, during some rare time off, Donnie sneaks away and goes to New York City with his road manager. There, he shops and makes the club scene.

Donnie's sentimental side comes out when he talks about his new nephew, Adam.

JON SECRETS

When he's home, he still goes shopping with his mom.

His older brother David has his own band

called Homework; they're working with Maurice Starr.

Along with Jordan, he bought his mom a new home. It's outside Boston, on a hill overlooking the Atlantic Ocean, surrounded by trees. The entire family will live there together.

Jon hates messes; it's he who keeps the tour bus neat.

He's a "do-it-yourselfer," preferring to mow the lawn and make repairs himself rather than hire someone to do it for him.

He graduated from high school but probably will not go to college right now.

Because the group is sometimes in a different hotel each night, Jon tends to forget what room he's in. That's a problem when he loses his key, which he's prone to do; he can't remember what to ask for when he goes to the front desk!

Jon hates when people make comparisons between New Kids and other groups.

He planted a white dogwood tree in the family's front yard last year. When he came home from the tour, he found that overzealous fans had pulled the branches off. Patient Jon nursed it back to health.

He still has his childhood fear of the dark!

He still suffers from stage fright *and* is still shaky about the thought of soloing.

He's right-handed.

He took a hiatus from high school for a

while; Jordan, although younger, actually graduated first.

Jon started at Boston's English High School, but because the group was on the road and he had to have a tutor, he couldn't fulfill the graduation requirements there; he ended up getting his diploma from Catholic Memorial instead.

Jon's favorite food: chocolate chip cookies.

He's very concerned about how he looks when he's out in public. The other guys used to tease him, calling him "Mr. GQ," after the famous men's fashion magazine. Jon admits his biggest indulgence is buying clothes.

JORDAN SECRETS

He fell sound asleep in the middle of the movie *Batman*.

His mom still takes him to the orthodontist (yes, Jordan wears braces).

His pet project is producing an album for New Kids' opening act, Tommy Page.

Jordan's musical taste changes with his mood. He listens to jazz, rap and oldies.

One of his quirks: He "borrows" Jon's jackets and then leaves all his own stuff in the pockets; it drives Jon crazy.

He's got both ears pierced.

He's left-handed.

He graduated from Catholic Memorial High School.

He looks through all the gifts that fans send and tries to keep as many as possible.

Jordan's nervous habits: He bites his nails and twirls his hair.

Originally, he sang most of the leads, now it's more evenly divided.

He's secretly shopping for his own apartment in New York City.

He puts ketchup on everything!

His most prized possession is his keyboards.

He admits that his room at home is "very messy."

He collects hotel room keys.

He once forgot his line of a rap song during a live radio broadcast.

When he has some rare time off at home, Jordan enjoys spending it alone, just thinking and sorting things out.

He also spends as much time as possible hanging out with his old friends, driving around the city.

Jordan's scared of supernatural things.

DANNY SECRETS

He cries sometimes, especially when the pressure of being a New Kid gets to him.

He likes to sleep late.

He admits that he's always been stubborn but, lately, has learned to curb that hot temper he used to have.

He knows how to handle his own laundry; that's one of the things he always had to do as a kid.

When he left college, before New Kids really took off, he worked briefly as a messenger, delivering airline tickets. He quit when "Please Don't Go Girl" came out.

Offstage, he wears glasses.

The Shining is the scariest movie he's ever seen.

When he's home, he likes to spend his evenings hanging out "with the homeboys," that is, his old friends.

His oldest sister, Bethany, recently got married.

He has a niece named Danielle.

He's right-handed.

Danny wears a gold musical G-clef earring.

Once, he came home from a tour and found that his mom had given away nearly all his clothes to fans who'd come to the door asking for a souvenir!

Although Danny still lives in his childhood home, it was recently remodeled. He now has his own apartment on a newly added third floor.

His favorite kind of music is anything and everything Maurice Starr writes and produces.

He's getting college credit while on the road with New Kids.

JOE SECRETS

Little Joe is quite the impressionist. He does "dead-on" impressions of each New Kid and really cracks them up. He used to entertain his family by imitating his eight siblings.

He hates to lose at anything!

Although he looks through and appreciates all the gifts that fans send, he's given most of them away to kids in hospitals.

Now that he's got a driver's license, Joe likes to rent convertibles.

Joe's quirk: He makes funny faces when he thinks no one is looking.

His mother *always* calls him Joseph.

His friends always call him Joey!

Joe is very proud of his mom, who recently lost a great deal of weight. Now, he doesn't like to see photos of her printed from before the weight loss.

Of all the New Kids, Joe misses home the most when they're on the road.

His first ambition was to be a bricklayer, just like his dad.

Joe's quote about New Kids: "We're just like everyone else, dreamers. We are the middle American boys next door."

SECRETS OF THEIR SUCCESS

Why have New Kids been so successful—and why will they stay that way? They're all grounded in family values. They feel like blood relatives of one another's *and* of their entire management and crew. They'd do anything for one another.

They're nice people! They say, "The reason we do this is to make people happy. It's not just a business thing, to make money."

They don't take all their success for granted. They understand how lucky they are; they understand that they are pampered. They work hard not to let it all go to their heads.

All their families are involved with the group on one level or another. Their moms are still executive directors of the fan club and review everything that goes out to fans.

They give credit where it's due, especially to Mary Alford, their original manager, and Maurice Starr, the man who groomed them, and who writes and produces much of their music. Donnie speaks for the entire group when he says, "We're very close to Maurice. He's been a very good teacher. When I started out I had never sung before. I was scared. I had no confidence in my singing. But he gave me confidence, he built me up. He built us all up. He made us feel like we could do anything. His confidence in us has been incredible. Without it, I don't think we could have made it."

They care seriously about each and every performance. Because they were unhappy with their performance on this year's televised "American Music Awards," they postponed one for "The Dance Music Awards" so they could polish their TV act.

They aren't frittering away the money they're making. New Kids' finances are all managed and invested carefully by a prominent Boston law firm. They won't be left high and dry when their glory days are over—which, of course, won't be for a long, long time!

8

Life on the Road

NEW KIDS SPEND SO MUCH TIME "ON THE ROAD"—
that is, traveling from city to city—to bring
their outrageous music to you, it's truly a
lifestyle all its own. Have you ever wondered
what it's really like for Donnie, Danny, Jon,
Jordan and Joe? Well, hop on the tour bus,
here's your private behind-the-scenes glimpse
of life on the road with the "fab five."

The first thing to grasp is what concerts are
all about—why, when and where the guys
actually do them. The idea, of course, is to
bring the Kids and their music to *your* block,
to give fans a live, up-close-enough-to-touch
experience with the group. Better than listen-

ing to them on the radio, better than seeing them on TV or in your favorite magazine, concerts are the place where you can *really* get to see and know the guys in person. For most fans, it's the closest they'll ever get.

In concert, the group will sing not only all their hits but also other tracks from their albums, plus new tunes as well. But that's not all they do. For concerts are the places where each member gets to talk and have some fun with the audience, letting *you* in on their true, fun-loving personalities.

Concert tours can be long or short, stopping at many cities and towns or just a few. It really all depends on the demand, on how many fans in how many cities really want to see them! Naturally, in New Kids' case, concert tours have been very, very long. Since *Hangin' Tough* came out in 1988, Donnie, Danny, Jon, Jordan and Joe have been on the road nearly three-quarters of each year since! They go to the cities where fans want them and play in an area concert hall, arena or stadium, referred to as the "venue."

In general, an act will go "on the road" right after an album is released to give fans a sampling of the songs on that record or, as it's called in the business, to "promote" the album. The hope is that they'll already have at least one hit single being played on the radio, so audiences will be familiar with the material.

New Kids' fans, of course, generally know all the songs on the albums and just can't wait to hear the new stuff.

There's no question that millions of fans all over the world want New Kids in their towns, but how do the boys feel about all that performing? Are you kidding? According to them, that's the best part of being a New Kid! "Being able to go on stage, in front of twenty thousand people, and perform, and hear all the girls screaming, is absolutely the best part of it all," they agree. The sheer joy of performing their music live is the greatest, performing it for their adoring fans is the icing on the cake. Anyone who's seen New Kids in concert *knows* the guys are having the time of their lives up on stage—and that joy is infectious. No girl leaves a New Kids concert without a great big smile on her face!

But aside from that hour and a half up on stage, Donnie, Danny, Jon, Jordan and Joe really like traveling. They enjoy seeing different places and are proud to say they've been to forty-nine states plus several foreign countries. Not too often, but every once in a while, there's a "window of opportunity" built into their schedule for a mini-vacation. This year, they spent three restful days in Florida right before their Grammy Awards appearance—all their parents came down from Boston during that time to visit with them.

Being on the road, too, gives them the chance to meet many of their fans, and just as you want to meet them, the feeling is very much mutual. It's true that only a small percentage of fans get to meet the guys on a one-to-one basis (a bit later on in this chapter, you'll see how to increase your odds), but New Kids are grateful for even that. The guys not only want to know who their fans are and what they want, but they relish the opportunity, every single time, to personally say "thanks." These are five guys who truly understand the part their fans play in their continual success —and they're eternally grateful. Getting the chance to say thanks, in person, is one big reason they love to tour.

No matter how much they love it, no Kid would ever say that touring is easy. They're young, energetic and enthusiastic, but the pace can really be grueling. A typical day on the road might go something like this.

The tour bus brings them into town at six—in the morning, that is! They hit the hotel, freshen up for a bit, eat breakfast and then rehearse from about eleven A.M. to two P.M. At around four P.M., they'll go to the venue for a "sound check." That's where the Kids and the road crew check out the place, figure out the stage setup and make any last-minute adjustments in the upcoming show. In between, there might be interviews with the press, meetings, photo sessions and possibly recording sessions as well. From five-thirty to seven P.M., they'll have dinner and get ready for the show, which may start around eight P.M. and end close to eleven P.M. After the show (as you'll see later), the Kids get to meet fans and other important people in each town, open gifts, sign autographs and possibly squeeze in some time with a visiting friend or relative. Sometimes, they don't get back to the hotel until the wee hours of the morning—and often there are fans in the lobby wanting autographs. And because New Kids are who they are, and in spite of how bushed they are, often as not they'll try to oblige.

Many nights, they don't hit the sack until three A.M.—and get up again at six, because there's another gig to get to in another town. Yes, it's exhausting . . . but they wouldn't trade it for anything.

Getting There: The Tour Bus

They've got a concert in Cleveland tonight and another in Pittsburgh tomorrow. The day after it's Cincinnati, and two days after *that,* they're due in Chicago. New Kids travel from city to city by bus, three great big buses, that is, designed expressly for them. Many performers travel this way, though the more established acts generally opt to fly. Not that the Kids aren't established or can't afford private planes, but the truth is that the Kids like their tour buses—as well they should!

"They're just like home," Donnie explains, "with a living room, refrigerator, bedrooms, bathrooms and lots of things to do. We love them!" New Kids tour buses are equipped with all the latest in fun: stereos, VCR, and lots of video games, sent complimentary by Nintendo. If they're not challenging each other on the games, they might be catching up on the latest movie. Although the bus is stocked with tons of cassettes, the boys usually opt for an Eddie Murphy comedy.

The tour bus is the place they often get to open and inspect all the gifts fans send to the hotel or toss up onstage at the concert itself. Although they can't always keep everything—they donate most of it to hospitals—they do try and see that everyone who sends a gift gets some sort of thank you.

Jordan always has his keyboards with him on the bus and he's often off by himself, tinkering away or perhaps reading a book. Jon sometimes noodles on his bass guitar; it's Donnie who raids the fridge more often than not!

All five Kids aren't on the same bus. Brothers Jon and Jordan Knight travel together on one, while Donnie, Danny and Joe are on another. The third one is for the Kids' road crew and other people who travel with them, including their road manager Peter Work, bodyguards Biscuit and Robo and Perry plus their tutor Mark. Those long drives between cities give them all a chance to talk and "brainstorm" about the concert they just played and what's upcoming. The tour bus is the place the guys come up with some of their best ideas!

Want to know the real secret of what New Kids on the Block do on their private tour buses? Jon lets the cat out of the bag: "Eighty percent of the time, we sleep! We jump into our bunk beds, each of us has a teddy bear, and the motion of the bus just kinda rocks us to sleep!"

Hotel Hijinks

As the buses rumble into each city, they pull up to a hotel and the whole entourage checks in. Reservations have been made way in advance, and, usually, the hotel is well prepared. That is, an entire floor is generally reserved for New Kids and their crew; that floor is sealed off by security guards from every possible entrance. That's because no matter how secretive the New Kids staff is, fans always figure out which hotel they're at and try all sorts of ingenious methods to get to them. It isn't that the guys don't want to meet their fans, but once word spreads, a riot could start, and no one wants that.

In the good old days, the Kids used to share rooms; now, each one has his own, and though they have lots of space, those rooms are usually pretty messy. Reporters who've come to interview them nearly always comment on the crumpled socks left lying around and the half-eaten burgers on the floor.

That's the worst that can be said about New Kids' hotel behavior, though. While many rock bands on the road have reputations for trashing their hotel rooms, New Kids don't. They may wrestle with each other and have the occasional playful water fight to let off steam, but they basically respect the property of others and have never destroyed anything.

So what do they do in the hotel? Phone home, sleep (the Knight brothers get the award for latest sleepers) and order lots of room service. A typical New Kids order will include hot dogs, hamburgers, fries, potato salad and chips—these growing Kids need lots of energy, and this is one way of getting it!

How to Increase Your Chances of Meeting Them

Naturally, the dream of every New Kid fan is to meet her idol, and what more obvious time to try than when the Kids are appearing in her city? Sounds do-able, but since thousands of fans have the exact same idea, it isn't easy. It can be done, but it takes planning, inside info and lots of luck! Here's some inside info.

You have to know where they'll be or at least where they're most likely to be. That means first figuring out the hotel they'll be staying at. It's likely to be a big expensive hotel; it's likely to be fairly close to the venue they'll be performing at. If they've played in your city before, chances are they're at the same place they stayed at last time, but calling the hotel and asking will not get you an answer (though you could try, you never know). Radio stations will know, the local press will probably know, the concert promoter will know. Sometimes, you can find out just by an ear to the grapevine —with a little detective work, finding the hotel is usually pretty easy.

What do you do once you've figured out where they'll be? Frankly speaking, your best bet—with your parents, of course—is to check in a day or two earlier to the same hotel. Being a guest will entitle you to the same facilities as the Kids and, frankly, that's your best shot at finding them. But spending money on a hotel bill is not a real practical way for most fans to meet the New Kids. Finding a way to be at the hotel during the time they're there, however, could result in that long-dreamed-of meeting.

You can figure that the Kids will probably arrive in town early in the day of the concert, so being in the lobby of the hotel that day—with one or two friends, not a whole crowd—might find you face to face with Jordan or Jon or Donnie or Danny or Joe, or maybe all of them, if you're really lucky! Aside from that possibility, knowing their hotel haunts will help, too. For instance, though they often order room service, every once in a while a Kid will come to the hotel restaurant or coffee shop to chow down. Several elated fans have met one or two of them there. Danny Wood, the exercise nut, might very well bc in the weight or exercise room of the hotel—any one of them might be in the hotel swimming pool. Don't forget the video game arcades and pool tables at the hotel, and if the hotel has basketball courts or mini golf (some of the biggest ones do), that's a good bet for finding them.

The time before they rush out to a concert is not a good time to be in the lobby; the time before they head out for a sound check (usually, about four in the afternoon) is a better idea. They may not be as rushed and can take a few minutes to stop and say "hi." Some fans stake out the hotel lobby late at night after a concert, but most parents understandably aren't too thrilled with that idea. Besides, the guys are usually totally exhausted at that point.

How do the guys feel about fans hanging out at the hotel? They're real candid and say that they're usually instructed not to stop and talk to fans because it disrupts the other guests. But that advice isn't always taken by the Kids! They love their fans and find it hard to ignore them. Jordan says, "We appreciate them following our career and supporting us. It's important to all of us to make our fans feel good, because we know that without them, we would have nothing."

So going against advice, more often than not, Jordan, Jon, Donnie, Danny and Joe stop and sign autographs in the hotel lobby, or at the very least, hang out the window of their rooms, waving at the throngs of frenzied fans on the street. They admit that it's easier when they're not all together, and so every once in a while one Kid might come bouncing down the stairs to say "hi." Jordan reveals that he especially likes meeting and hanging out with fans away from the other guys and away from the crowds, on a one-to-one basis.

Do the guys ever get away from the hotel—before or after a concert—and hang out in any other places in town? It's rare, they have very little time, but on occasion they do. You might find a Kid at a local shopping mall (pick the most upscale one around), or if there's a big amusement park in the area, they love going on the rides. On their first tour, with Tiffany, when they weren't quite as well known, they used to hit all the amusement parks all over the country. That's not so easy to do now, because they cause chaos wherever they go— and the Kids are not into wearing disguises when they go out.

Every once in a while they'll even go to a movie theater in town, but more often than not, they'll rent out the entire theater!

Other possibilities for meeting them: You know they must do a sound check before each concert. That means they'll be at the venue late in the afternoon, checking out the facilities. If you go there, you'll know if they're there by all the equipment trucks and limousines parked outside. You might catch them coming or going—and if they see you, if they possibly can, they will come over.

The truth is that the Kids delight in meeting their fans, and best of all for them is actually surprising fans by running into them unexpectedly. Once, they were at an office building for a meeting (business meetings are something the Kids might be doing in cities like Boston, Los Angeles, New York and Chicago) and spied some girls wearing New Kids T-shirts in the parking lot. The girls didn't see them (who'd be looking for them in an office-building parking lot?), but that didn't stop the guys from walking right up and talking to the surprised fans. "It makes you feel so good," they say, "to know you can make a girl's day by just shaking her hand, saying "hi" or giving a hug. That's something special."

Problems on the Road

Of course, it's not all fun and games on the road, even for New Kids. There's a downside to all that travel and the candid Kids are the first to admit it. "It's tiring" is the first thing they say about the negatives of touring and you can see that keeping up the pace they do is exhausting. "We only sleep four or five hours a night," they remind you, and as much as they love their tour buses, they're not nearly as comfortable as their good old beds at home.

And speaking of home, after a few weeks out roaming the hinterlands, they miss it! Joe especially still suffers from bouts of homesickness, and all the guys miss their friends and families. For that reason, New Kids managers have equipped each Kid with a beeper, so they know if someone from home is trying to reach them. And as you might expect, all of them phone mom every single day.

Another problem on the road is that when things get really hectic, even the Kids' good-natured nerves get frayed. There are times when they snap at each other and even get sick of one another! "It's like any other set of friends," Danny explains. "We get along great sometimes and other times we have our disagreements." Jon adds, "Sometimes we have to fight to get along!"

Experience has taught them that when problems arise, they should talk it out in order to solve them. "If you have a problem with someone," Joe says, "you should tell them, instead of exploding later on. So we talk a lot, communicate a lot and that helps." It's a lesson that serves them well.

It's Showtime!

Of course, none of the negatives comes close to overshadowing the excitement and joy of putting on a show for you. The concert itself is the reason they're on the road and those hours up on the stage are worth everything to New Kids.

Usually, the boys arrive at the venue an hour or so before they're scheduled to go on. While their opening acts are on the stage, Jon, Jordan, Joe, Danny and Donnie are backstage, in their dressing rooms getting ready—and getting excited. They drink a special blend of honey lemon tea to soothe their throats, get into the first of several outfits they'll perform in, fix their hair with lots of hairspray. They loosen up by wrestling with each other and fooling around; Jordan might grab a nearby guitar and crack everyone up with his Elvis impersonation.

The energy's high and so's the creativity backstage. Although much of what they're about to do onstage is totally improvised, before the show the boys often get a hot idea and you'll hear them exclaiming, "Oh, this would look good if we did it this way." Or about a dance step: "They'd go crazy if we did this . . ." New Kids want to please the audience and they know just how to do it!

"Onstage is the best time of our lives," the Kids agree. "We have so much fun." And when they finally get there, after (usually) two opening acts and an intermission, it's obvious that these Kids live to perform. And as the lights dim and twenty thousand deafening screams pierce the air, the Kids take the stage to the blasting rhythms of their tight 'n fresh backup band. Under the lasers and spotlights, they're all over the stage, moving and grooving to the beat of their opening number, "My Favorite Girl."

Switching leads, trading quips and friendly punches, breakdancing breathlessly to dazzling choreography, the Kids caress the love songs, such as "Please Don't Go Girl" and "I'll Be Loving You (Forever)," dish out the rockers, such as "Whatcha Gonna Do About It," and lead the audience in the moves that go to "The Right Stuff."

Devoted fans know every word and each step, and the Kids never disappoint for a second. They stop the music to really talk to the audience and let them know how much they're loved. In Donnie's rendition of "Cover Girl," he sometimes takes a shocked fan out of the audience to come up on the stage, so he can sing, on bended knee, just to her. It's a dream come true for the chosen fan who's usually too overwhelmed to do anything but stand there!

Twice during the show, they run backstage where tents are set up as makeshift dressing rooms and quickly switch outfits from the dazzling glitter they've started out in, to rough 'n tough leather jackets and jeans that work better with the rockers.

The Kids play instruments during the "New Kids groove"; holding hands high in the air, they slow the pace altogether for the moving "This One's for the Children." They never seem to want to leave the stage, they're having so much fun up there, but eventually they do. As the audience screams for more, the music plays and, as long as the lights are still down, the fans know the Kids will come out for an encore.

But what an encore! As they run in from the wings, a catwalk is lowered from the ceiling and stops at the lip of the stage—the Kids jump on it and swing out over the audience, dancing and singing "Hangin' Tough!" For the encore, they often make one more costume change—into T-shirts bearing the name of the city they're in.

As the show comes to a close, the Kids stay onstage, hands joined, bowing, waving, grinning, blowing kisses to the audience. Sometimes, Jordan will toss a hat out and fans will toss gifts up that will be taken backstage or put on the tour bus. New Kids leave no doubt that they love their fans and they love performing for them.

When the Show Is Over . . .

At concert's end, the boys dash backstage in high gear. They're congratulated by the crew, bodyguards, their managers and producers who go to most of their shows. But while most bands, still flying high from the rush of being onstage, go out and party after a gig, the New Kids do something else. They almost always adjourn to a special room backstage that's set up in nearly every town called "The Meet and Greet Room." That's the place and that's the time they've set aside for officially meeting fans. The lucky ones who get to wait for them in the Meet and Greet Room are usually contest winners (set up by the local radio stations or newspapers or magazines or the promoter) or possibly the sons and daughters of people influential in the town and all their friends.

Sometimes, the New Kids fan club has contest winners who get to meet the band, and every once in a while, someone who's written them a particularly moving letter might be sent a backstage pass.

Why do the Kids set aside this special time to go out of their way to shake hands with as many fans as possible? Because it's part of being nice, and that's what the New Kids are all about!

9

The Flipside

It's easy to see all the wonderful and exciting things about being part of New Kids on the Block, so easy, in fact, you might not think there's any downside to it at all. But there's where you'd be wrong. For although the positives certainly outweigh the negatives, still there are a few things that Donnie, Danny, Jon, Jordan and Joe would change, if they could.

"I thought all of this would be easy. I thought it would be like pie. I really did." Jordan Knight said that, with a resigned sigh in his voice, not so very long ago. What Jordan realized is that (as a rock group put it in a popular song) "every rose has its thorn." Here are some of the thorns New Kids on the Block have been pricked with.

"We Can't Be Normal"

Donnie Wahlberg, Danny Wood, Joe McIntyre and Jon and Jordan Knight are five of the most normal Kids you'll ever meet. They come from average, hardworking families and are used to the simple pleasures of normal life: going to the mall, hanging out with their friends, going to the movies—everyday things you take for granted. They can't do those things anymore—not unless they want to start a riot, that is! For they're so famous now that any time a New Kid is recognized, at a restaurant or just walking down the block, he's instantly mobbed. Try to imagine what that's like. Maybe the first one or two times it would be fun, but after that, it's really hard to deal with.

Jon relays an example of a time he expected some privacy, but didn't get it. "I was at a hotel one time, just relaxing in the Jacuzzi. Suddenly, all these girls came running into the hotel and they all stood around watching me in the Jacuzzi. I was so embarrassed. I felt like a fish in the aquarium!"

There are times when even the New Kids just don't feel they're looking that great, or simply need some quiet "down" time. That's especially true for creative people; they need alone time to create that music, write those lyrics, think up those dynamic dance steps. For the New Kids, the only time they're really alone is late at night in their hotel rooms—by then, they're usually too tired to be real creative!

Aside from their own personal needs, however, creating mob scenes wherever they go leads to security problems. And the Kids aren't even worried so much about themselves, as the possibility of their fans getting hurt. That's why they must go *everywhere* with big burly bodyguards and, when they perform, employ a major security force. In fact, there's a clause written into their performance contracts that stipulates each venue must supply ten additional security guards at each show, aside from the ones New Kids bring!

The New Kids don't only have almost no time alone, they have almost no *time,* period! If they're not rehearsing, they're recording; if they're not recording, they're performing. And they're always traveling somewhere, for something. Jon's example: "On our last tour, we had two days off on the East Coast, but we had to fly to San Francisco for a promotional show. Then, we turned around and flew all the way back to the East Coast in time for the next show. Another time we were in four different states in the day!"

Their head-spinning schedule leaves little time to spend with their families, and for five Kids who are so attached to theirs, that's a major hardship. They aren't just pretending to be family-oriented guys, they really *are!*

The Rumor Mill

Another inescapable fact of life for the New Kids and other celebrities: When you're famous, rumors crop up about you and spread like wildfire. Some are just plain laughably *wrong,* others are downright hurtful, while some actually have a grain of truth to them, but get twisted out of proportion. Living with rumors is hard enough for the Kids, it's worse for their families, who are often thousands of miles away and don't know what to believe.

Here are some (for it's impossible to keep up with *all*) of the rumors spread about New Kids, and here's the truth about them.

Donnie's quitting the group.

Actually, you could put anyone's name in there, for the rumor that *someone's* leaving seems to crop up every single day. For some reason, Donnie's is the name that comes up most often. It's not true, at least not for now!

No one can predict what will happen in the future, but none of the Kids has any plans to leave.

Donnie's dating Betty from Sweet Sensation.

Donnie doesn't have a steady girlfriend. Of course, he's friends with all the ladies in Sweet Sensation, one of New Kids' opening acts, but there's no romance there.

New Kids made their debut on TV's "Star Search."

They've never been on "Star Search."

The group saved Jordan from a career in graffiti vandalism.

This one popped up in an English tabloid and is just an example of how things get exaggerated way out of proportion. Jordan admits to having been something of a graffiti artist, way back when, but he's not a vandal. Besides, Jordan Knight would have made a success of his life with or without New Kids.

The girls in their videos are their real girlfriends.

The girls in their videos are actresses and models who, for the most part, the guys don't even know.

They've been terrorized by death threats.

So one American tabloid reported. Anyone in the public eye is subject to threats by lunatics, but the Kids are well protected and don't spend a lot of time worrying about that fringe element.

The rock group Skid Row got into a fight with New Kids.

The two groups have never met.

Tiffany and Jon Knight are secretly married and about to be parents.

This is an example of one that's blown totally out of proportion. Tiffany and Jon are going together, they're not secretly married, they're not expecting.

New Kids will star in a movie.

This one happens to be true—in the next chapter you'll find out more.

Jordan has a secret girlfriend.

Again, you can substitute any name here. Jordan, Joe and Donnie do not have girlfriends. Jon does; Danny might.

They give all the gifts from fans to charity.

The boys appreciate to no end the fact that their lovin' fans give them presents. They look through them all, they try to thank each and every gift-giver, they try to keep some of them. But the boys have big hearts and want to share their good fortune with kids in hospitals who are less fortunate than they are. So, yes, a lot of the presents they receive do end up in hospitals or with charitable organizations.

Jordan got a broken rib in a fight; Donnie has terrible bruises.

New Kids are lovers, not fighters; they're all fine.

Joe told reporters that he wants a petite girlfriend and wouldn't date a bigger girl.

Joe McIntyre would date anyone he liked, regardless of physical appearance. Like the other New Kids, he doesn't judge anyone by their looks.

Jordan has a dread disease.

This one seems to be a stock rumor that surfaces about anyone in the public eye. All the New Kids are healthy and happy!

Jon and Jordan hate their father.

It's doubtful that Jon and Jordan hate anyone, but the situation with their dad is complicated and very private. The boys admit that they have no contact with Allan Knight, who has remarried, but choose not to elaborate further. And you have to respect their privacy.

As they reach a certain age, the New Kids are going to "trade out," like Menudo, and get new, younger members.

This one's really ridiculous. The group has had the same five members since 1985, no one's being "traded."

Jonathan Knight is color blind and Jordan has to help him pick out his clothes.

Jonathan can see just fine, he's not color blind. Both, however, give their opinions about the other one's clothes!

Four of the New Kids smoke, everyone but Joe.

None of the New Kids smokes!

Jordan and Joe are fighting.

Except for an occasional squabble (which is normal, considering they spend so much time together), none of the Kids is fighting. And if anyone were, it wouldn't be Jordan: He's the most easygoing Kid on the block!

Who's "Dissin'" the New Kids?

"Dissin'" is a street term for being disrespectful, and there are people out there who, for one reason or another, just don't like the Kids and publicly say things about them that hurt. The New Kids backlash is no doubt due to plain old jealousy, but still the verbal attacks sting the boys.

They've been accused of not playing their own instruments. The Kids don't dispute the fact that when they joined the group, they didn't have to. They had to be able to sing, move and have great personalities; they didn't have to be musicians. Many big musical stars don't play instruments onstage or on their records—Michael Jackson, for instance—and no one accuses them of being any less talented or professional. In truth, the guys are learning instruments now. They play a little in concert and will play more on their next tour. What bothers them more than that accusation, however, is not being taken seriously by music-industry people who call them "just a teeny-bopper act." The Kids feel they do make a viable contribution to the world of popular music—and certainly the more than seven million fans who bought *Hangin' Tough* seem to agree! Still, everyone wants to be recognized by their peers, and it rankles New Kids when they're not.

It's been said that they're "puppets" of Maurice Starr. He, along with Mary Alford, discovered them, groomed them and tells them exactly what to say and how to act. This kind of talk really upsets the Kids. They know they owe a lot to their genius producer, and they give him all the credit in the world, but they're no one's puppets, not in the recording studio, on the stage, in public or in private. They were all very young when the band first came to be, and, of course, they followed Maurice's lead— he taught them a lot musically. But these days, the savvy Kids have a great deal of input into their albums and their concerts. And their personalities are all their own: No one tells them what to say and how to act. What you see and hear is what you get!

MTV stopped playing their videos, because they wanted to attract an older audience. What an irony! MTV, after all, is what helped launch the New Kids in the first place: A radio deejay saw one of their videos on MTV and knew right away the Kids were going to be popular, so he started playing their records on the air. That's what kicked it all off for New Kids. Suddenly, MTV decided to kick them off the air. It's all part of not being taken seriously as a musical act and that really hurts the Kids. Naturally, there was an outpouring of protest when MTV made its decision—New Kids fans won't stand by and see their band being treated like that!

They're the butt of jokes. While that's true,

the Kids have come to understand that so is *anyone* as famous as they are. They even thought the Christmas parody song about them, "New Kids Got Run Over by a Reindeer," a silly ditty that actually made the Top 40 last year, was funny. Developing a sense of humor about all the sniping and backlash is how they've learned to deal with it all—or with most of it, at least!

They can't please everyone. This is something they've also come to understand, but when it involves their fans, the boys find it hard to accept. "We really try to please everyone," they say, "but when hundreds of kids run up to us and want autographs, we don't always have the time, and they don't always understand." It seems that as much as they do, it's never enough. And since the Kids don't like to disappoint anyone, they have a hard time with that.

What They Worry About

Although they don't let the downside of being a New Kid get to them too often, they do worry about certain things. One of them, believe it or not, is overexposure. It may seem to you that there could never be too much of the fab five, but they're concerned about a New Kids overdose! After all, they've had three albums on the Top 100 chart at the same time, and they have had one hit single after another for a year, without a break. They're afraid people will get sick of them! "We don't want to put too many singles out," they say. "We purposely want some time with no New Kids music on the radio!"

Aside from being on the radio constantly, the Kids have been in concert all over the USA, and it seems, every time you turn around, they're on one TV program or another. Not to mention being prominent cover boys on *every* teen magazine in existence, month after month!

Now the Kids don't plan on a disappearing act anytime soon, but they know full well that it's human nature to get tired of the "same old thing" and to be on the lookout for something, or someone, new. They hope you don't get tired of them!

Something else they worry about, and it's something of concern to all musicians, is stagnation. The Kids are anxious to grow creatively, not put out the same exact kind of music year after year. They understand that they have to keep growing and changing in order to stay successful *and* to be creatively fulfilled. And that's exactly what they plan on doing. "If not, we'll be has-beens," they say. And no one wants that!

You may find this hard to believe, but the Kids also worry about their *name*. How long, they wonder, can they be the New Kids on the Block? Somehow "Old Men on the Block" doesn't have the same ring to it!

To their fans, these worries may seem trivial: *You* know who they are and what they do and you'll always love them. And somewhere deep inside, Donnie, Danny, Jon, Jordan and Joe know that, too.

10

"This One's for the Children"

THERE'S MORE TO NEW KIDS THAN JUST THE FRESH-est music, smoothest moves, cutest faces and nicest personalities on the block. NKOTB has "the right stuff" in other ways, too. As a group, they have some very lofty ideals and they don't miss a chance to spread their lovin' message to kids all over. Simply put, they're dedicated to making their world—and yours—a better place to live in.

Because they're so popular, the Kids enjoy a high profile—that is, people know who they are and take what they have to say seriously. If New Kids say drugs are uncool, young people are more likely to believe it than if a teacher or parent said it. If New Kids do performances for charity, they may very well inspire their devoted fans to think about others less fortunate.

Donnie, Danny, Jon, Jordan and Joe take their "roles" as role models very seriously. "This is how we really are and we know our fans are our peers. We want to set a good image for them," Donnie explains. "We project our own image. We don't put out a fake image for people. We're just ourselves."

Jordan says, "The kids are the future and we gotta set the future on a good course." His brother Jon puts it simply: "We love to help people!"

You know that NKOTB aren't just rattling off trendy phrases when they rap about serious things like helping people, saying no to drugs and yes to racial harmony: They *live* what they believe. And the key to knowing them is seeing how they live and listening to what they say.

No one ever told the Kids that they should love people of all colors and backgrounds; no one ever had to tell them that "all people are created equal." No one preached that they shouldn't prejudge someone by the color of his skin or by the way she talks. Those are things they never even questioned, because that's how they were brought up. And they find it really strange that the whole world doesn't think the same way they do!

Jon explains, "We were all brought up not to ever judge people. First of all, we grew up in the city and went to school with people of mixed backgrounds. I never thought about it. We have an adopted brother, Chris, who happens to be black. The only thing that's weird is when people actually ask me how I feel about that! He's my brother, just like Jordan, and it never occurred to me to feel anything about it. What I do feel is badly for kids who don't get the chance to learn about other people and other ways of life."

Donnie feels just as strongly as Jon. "We started to go to school when busing started. This made us the people we are. We went to school with different races, and we were the minority. A lot of kids were Spanish and black. Other kids went to private school to avoid the busing, but that has its limitations. You become ignorant to other ways of life. You don't open up your mind."

The Kids aren't just repeating rhetoric: They not only have friends of all colors but also the people they feel *closest* to—their producer Maurice Starr, their managers, and most of their road crew—happen to be black. "This is our family," they say.

The Kids even feel that one of the reasons

they're successful today is *because* of their beliefs and early experiences. One inescapable fact is that if it weren't for being bused to school, Donnie and Danny might never have met each other or the Knight brothers!

The only kinds of people the Kids have trouble accepting are those who are prejudiced. "Prejudice causes people to jump to conclusions about others before even getting to know them," Danny says. "It goes beyond the color of a person's skin. Some people are prejudiced against teenagers, assuming that they're all mixed up with drugs or gangs."

The Kids feel very strongly that "people need to start smartening up because this is our world, we all have to share it and people need to learn to get along together."

Joe adds, "It's not what's out there that you have to worry about, it's what's in your heart and your head that matter."

Saying "No" to drugs is something NKOTB feels just as strongly about and are just as vocal about! And once again, when they talk about drugs, they're not just repeating platitudes— they speak from real nitty-gritty experience. Because they grew up on the tough city streets, they've seen the damage that drugs can do. None of the Kids ever gave in to the temptation, but, nevertheless, it was there. Donnie once admitted, "Yeah, I've lived, I've had drugs in my face; I have a brother who had a problem, a sister who experimented."

Jordan continues, "The neighborhood we come from is rough, it's inner city, lots of crime and drugs. We see people hanging out, standing on street corners, wasting their lives away using drugs. If *we* can survive, you can definitely survive."

Staying in school is one way of staying off the streets and away from the temptations of drugs. The Kids, who have all graduated from high school, understand the importance of that. "Everyone should try to finish school no matter what," says Danny, who's gone on to college. "Some people might think they're smart enough without school, but that piece of paper you get when you graduate, that diploma, means so much in the world today."

Danny adds, "If you're on the streets you're looking for trouble. Play sports, play music, find a hobby. Get off the streets because there isn't anything there for you."

Jon cautions, "If some sucker ever offers you drugs, just say 'NO'—you'll be glad you did."

The New Kids are part of the (Massachusetts) Governor's Alliance Against Drugs. They not only talk to kids about the dangers, but they routinely donate money to the cause, too. Joe McIntyre often appears in concert wearing a T-shirt that says, "Drug-free body."

"Everyone needs someone with them to

help them be strong enough to stand up against drugs," Donnie reflects. "Think of *us* as your someone."

Doing for others is part of the New Kids credo, too, and to that end they do as much as they can for charity. Because they're so popular, they're besieged with requests to raise money for every charitable organization you can think of—and some you probably didn't know existed. The Kids try to accommodate when they can.

They've been connected with United Cerebral Palsy even before they were famous, performing on that organization's yearly telethon and raising money for the past four years. The Kids are "National Teen Spokespeople" for Cerebral Palsy and do a lot to raise our consciousness about it. They go further by donating their own earnings. At this year's telethon, they set up a special New Kids 900 phone line, where *all* the profits, at $5 a call, went to UCP. All by themselves, they raised $200,000 in two days! They're planning on doing the same thing next year, but making each call $10; they'd love to double the amount raised!

The Kids don't stop there: Every day of the week, a portion of the proceeds from their regular—and very lucrative—900 phone number goes to fight cerebral palsy, too.

"We want to do even more charity work in the future," they say, and you can bet that they will.

Other issues the Kids have strong feelings about are fighting to end homelessness and helping to solve our air pollution problem. They're planning on getting more involved with these causes in the near future, too.

Perhaps the most important message New Kids have for their fans is helping you understand the importance of feeling good about yourself. That's where it all starts; you can't fight peer pressure, think for yourself or help to make the world better if you don't feel good about *you*.

Donnie advises, "People have to be strong for themselves and start to respect their own opinions, respect their own thoughts. Once people start doing that, the world's gonna be a better place. Kids have to say, 'I'm *me*. If you want to do drugs, that's *you*. That's not *me*.'" He adds, "Being an individual is the best thing to be. Don't give in to peer pressure, do what your heart tells you to do."

Jordan chimes in with, "Try to live a positive life and try as hard as you can to just put down the negatives. 'Cause if you think positive that's where it starts. If you think positive and put down the negatives, you can be a success."

It's Jon who relays their message in the most simple way: "Love yourself."

To New Kids' way of thinking, making the world a better place has first and foremost to do with peace, among people and among nations. Donnie doesn't wear peace medallions because it looks cool; his goal in life is "world peace."

In 1989, New Kids sent out a Christmas card to their friends and fans. The message on it was simple and came directly from their hearts. "Peace and Love to all the children of the world."

Step by Step
into the Future

NEW KIDS IN THE '90s. THAT HAS AN EXCITING ring to it and there's no question of *big-time* excitement ahead. Sure, they've had mondo success already, but you ain't seen nothin' yet! The Kids are gearing up for an all-out assault that'll take them and their awesome music and dancing onto screens both big and small, into shopping malls, concert halls *and* the hearts of fans all over the world!

A New Album!

It's all starting right now with the release of their newest album, *Step by Step*. A blockbuster follow-up to *Hangin' Tough* and *Merry,*

Merry Christmas, it's produced once again by their musical mentor, Maurice Starr. This time, however, the maestro had some help—in the form of Jordan Nathaniel Marcel Knight and Daniel William Wood. The boys took their turns behind the big multileveled console and made creative decisions about engineering, producing, instrumentation and harmonies. "Maurice promised us we'd have more and more input on each album, as we learned," Jordan said, and that's exactly what's happened. Chalk up *Step by Step*'s fresh sounds to just that input!

There's no question that this, album number four, is as chock-full of hit singles as the others were. But there's no question that it's a step forward for New Kids. The music takes what they've already done and goes just a bit further, putting a new spin on it. Every tune's an original; there are no remakes on *Step by Step*.

It was recorded mainly on the road during New Kids' last big tour, with the majority of the tracks laid down in Los Angeles in November. Not only did the Kids sing, each having a crack at the lead, but they also co-wrote many of the tunes. They talked about being able to play their instruments on the album, but this time around, anyway, they didn't get the chance: They were just too short on time. That's certainly something they'll look forward to for album number five! Even without the Kids playing on it, though, *Step by Step* reflects New Kids' musical talents more than any of their albums so far—and they can't wait to find out how their fans like it.

A New Tour!

Naturally, they plan a sizzling coast-to-coast tour to bring their fresh sounds directly to you. Summer will see Donnie, Danny, Jon, Jordan and Joe on the U.S. concert trail once again with a radical all-new show. They've got loads of ideas for more high-tech fun onstage and can't wait to kick it all off. They're also working on some awesome new choreography for this go-round: No one moves like the Kids do; the new shows are bound to be show-stoppers!

Because of the overwhelming demand for tickets, the Kids will bring their act to huge stadiums in cities all over the country, as opposed to regular-size concert halls; this time they'll be playing to upwards of fifty thousand fans at a time. Don't worry about it being impersonal though. If you know the Kids, you know they'll find a way to make each and every fan feel like they're singing directly to her.

And always, as they tour, there's the opportunity to meet them in person, either on an "official" basis, in their "meet and greet" rooms, *or* completely unexpectedly. You never can tell!

The love that New Kids spread has expanded beyond the shores of the USA, into Canada and across an ocean or two. In the true New Kids spirit of brotherhood, they've united young fans all over the world from England to Australia to Japan and all points in between.

Springtime finds our heroes across the sea, concertizing for their fans of many colors and tongues, who adore them just as much as we do. It proves beyond a doubt that music *is* the universal language—and no one speaks it better than NKOTB!

A New Movie!

New Kids at the *Movies* is also on tap for the '90s, and their first major motion picture is already on the drawing board. There's no exact title or even time frame, though they're hoping to film it by year's end (probably in Los Angeles) and have it ready for the summer of 1991. The Kids have some idea of the kind of movie they want to star in. "It has to have a great story line," they've agreed, "and not be a rip-off, just exploiting the fact that we're popular. We may not even play ourselves!" Although the Kids are fine natural actors, if they do end up playing different characters, they may decide to spend some time with a drama coach before they start filming.

They've been thinking about their movie for some time now. "Every time something weird or funny or memorable happens, we say, 'Remember that for the movie!' We've been putting our ideas on tape to save them," they reveal.

As you can imagine, just about every big-shot movie mogul in Hollywood tried to sign them up; the Kids decided to cast their cinematic lot with the team who produced *Batman,* Peter Guber and Jon Peters, of Columbia Pictures, in the hopes of bringing their fans a real big-screen blockbuster.

Whether the New Kids movie turns out to be a comedy, drama or action thriller, there's one thing you can count on: It will have lots of music plus an awesome soundtrack as well.

New Kids on TV!

Going big-time on the big screen doesn't mean blowing off the small screen: New Kids on *TV* is a definite go for 1990 and beyond. They've begun by signing up for an animated Saturday morning TV series, starting in the fall on ABC. Each episode will open with a live-action, fast-paced montage set against one of their hit songs and will end with New Kids in performance. In between, the cartoon Kids will get involved in one cliff-hanger adventure after another. The guys will have as much input as possible into the show; they're really excited about it!

Saturday morning is not the only TV date fans can expect with the Kids. They'll be popping up on all sorts of other programs as well, including the big Awards shows like the "American Music Awards," the "Grammys," "Dance Music Awards" and "People's Choice Awards," too. They've made a deal to have an occasional concert air live on Pay Per View TV, and the Disney Channel has scooped up rights to present full-length videos like their *Hangin' Tough Live in Concert.*

Though there's nothing firm right now, there's also a very good chance the Kids may star in their own prime-time special around the holiday season. A good bet would find them on ABC, the network that's airing their Saturday morning show. Now *that's* something to look forward to!

New Kids on Your Shopping List

New Kids will invade the *mall* this year, too. They'll be represented in a line of Hasbro toys that includes New Kids dolls. The plastic replicas look exactly like each Kid and they come complete with onstage and offstage outfits. They'll be available in the fall and are sure to be on lots of Christmas lists come December. The same company, Hasbro, is also putting out a line of New Kids radios and phones.

The JC Penney Company is the official merchandiser for a full line of New Kids clothes. In their "Rock 'n Roll Shop" department, they'll offer New Kids denim jackets, oversize T-shirts, sweatshirts, hats and buttons, too, so fans can proudly strut around their blocks, displaying their love for those Boston babes.

That's just the beginning. New Kids are planning to lend their name and images to a variety of products, which will be unveiled periodically through the year.

Naturally, they'll be keeping on top of their 900-number phone line, with updated messages and new announcements about contests to meet them and new ways to communicate with the guys. And, as always, a portion of the revenue from the 900 line is set aside for charity. It's a good feeling to know that when you reach out to New Kids, you're also reaching out to other kids in need.

Commercial Kids

There's no question that the Kids will align themselves with a big company that will probably sponsor their summer stadium tour. Early word had them hooked up with Pepsi, to the tune of a $5.5-million-dollar deal. But that doesn't look like it's going to materialize after all. As you can imagine, the Kids were approached by several major companies: Right now, the inside line has them signing with Coke. Until all the i's have been dotted and t's crossed, however, an official announcement won't be made. Count on it happening, though —and count on seeing New Kids on TV in at least two rockin' commercials.

Personal Plans

As a group, they've got enough on their professional plates to last through the first half of the decade; each Kid has some *individual* goals as well for the '90s.

Donnie Wahlberg plans on producing an album for some of his old high school buddies, a rap group called The Northside Posse. He's been working with them in his spare time for quite a while and hopes to have a record out this year. Donnie's also been looking into playing "big daddy producer" for other bands as well.

Perhaps most exciting on Donnie's musical agenda is helping his younger brother Mark break into the biz. Mark was a New Kid for a short time in the very beginning, until he changed his mind and dropped out. That, however, was *then;* now Mark, who's every bit as cute as Donnie, has decided to test the musical waters as a rapper. Donnie and New Kids' original manager Mary Alford are working with Mark.

Rap music has always been Donnie's first love, and he's made no big secret of the fact that he dreams of one day making a rap album—all by himself. That doesn't mean he'd leave New Kids, just that he'd like to fulfill himself creatively with an occasional outside project.

On the personal side, Donnie-the-good-son has bought his mom a brand-new home just outside of Boston and is looking into a property for his dad. And what about himself? "I see myself with a house one day, a wife and a small family. But not for another five to ten years!"

The Knight brothers have also bought their mom a lovely new home and are looking forward to spending the next several years enjoying it with her. On the musical front, Jordan would like to expand his talents as a producer, not only for New Kids but also for other acts as well. His first project is a record with singer Tommy Page, and, so far, the collaboration has been real successful, resulting in a hit record for Tommy!

Jordan hopes to spend the next decade doing more behind-the-scenes work, writing songs and possibly, like Donnie, coming out with his own solo album. "I'd like for New Kids to have more platinum albums in the '90s—and for us to have fun," Jordan adds.

Big brother Jon Knight's goals are pure and simple: "To do my best in whatever I do!"

Danny Wood is pretty clear about what he hopes to do in the next decade: become a top-notch engineer and songwriter, work for other bands *and* for New Kids!

Joe McIntyre, only seventeen, looks forward to "learning more behind-the-scenes stuff about the music biz, and learning to become a producer like Maurice Starr. Maybe one day I'd even start a group like New Kids!" On a more personal level, little Joe can't wait to buy a car and make use of that brand-new driver's license he just got!

Whatever the '90s bring for New Kids on the Block, musically, dramatically and personally, there's one goal they'll continue to work toward as vigorously as ever: spreading their message *against* prejudice and *for* drug-free bodies, clean air, self-esteem and reaching out to help anyone in need. And as always, as a group, as individuals, as celebrities and as private citizens, to continue to work for peace, for all the children of the world.

That's what New Kids on the Block are really all about: Now you know.

Handy Addresses

Want to reach The Kids? Here are some places their mail goes.

New Kids on the Block
P.O. Box 7001
Quincy, MA 02269

New Kids on the Block Offical Fan Club
P.O Box 7080
Quincy, MA 02269

Columbia Records
51 W. 52nd Street
New York, NY 10019

Big Step Management
159 W. 53rd Street
New York, NY 10019

New Kids Lingo

Here are some words that the Kids use a lot—and here's what they mean:

Chill, or *chillin',* means staying loose, hanging back, relaxing!

Dis means disrespectful. To "dis" someone is to say something negative about that person.

Dude is a guy, a friend.

Homeboy is a friend from the neighborhood.

Go ill is to be cool.

Posse is a backup band, or group of friends.

It's dope means it's good!

New Kids Discography

New Kids on the Block, Columbia Records. Released April, 1986; re-released, 1989.
    Singles: "Be My Girl"
              "Stop It Girl"
              "Didn't I (Blow Your Mind)
    Popsicle
    Angle
    New Kids on the Block
    Are You Down?
    I Wanna Be Loved by You
    Don't Give Up on Me
    Treat Me Right

New Kids on the Block—Hangin' Tough, Columbia Records, 1988.

Singles: "Please Don't Go Girl"
  "(You Got It) The Right Stuff"
  "I'll Be Lovin' You (Forever)"
  "Hangin' Tough"
  "Cover Girl"
I Need You
I Remember When
What'cha Gonna Do (About It)
My Favorite Girl
Hold On

New Kids on the Block—Merry, Merry Christmas, Columbia Records, 1989.
  Single: "This One's for the Children"
  Last Night I Saw Santa Claus
  I'll Be Missin' You Come Christmas (A Letter to Santa)
  I Still Believe in Santa Claus
  Merry, Merry Christmas
  The Christmas Song (Chestnuts Roasting on an Open Fire)
  Funky, Funky Xmas
  White Christmas
  Little Drummer Boy
  This One's for the Children (Reprise)

New Kids on the Block—Step by Step, Columbia Records, 1990.

New Kids Videography

Music Videos: Please Don't Go Girl
You Got It (The Right Stuff)
I'll Be Lovin' You (Forever)
Hangin' Tough

Full Length Video Cassettes
New Kids on the Block—Hangin' Tough
(CBS Home Video, 1989)
New Kids on the Block—Hangin' Tough Live
in Concert (CBS Home Video, 1989)